I0524149

The Writer's Story

A Novel

Cory J. Schulman

Maryland

Best Seller Publications, LLC
Bestsellerpublications.com

This work is fiction. All main and incidental characters originated from the author's imagination and are used fictitiously. Any resemblance to actual persons, living or dead, is unintended.

Book design by Lori Schulman

ISBN: 978-0-9962344-7-4

Printed in the USA

Other Books Published by BestSellerPublications.com

FICTION

Textbook Follies
A Postcard from Jerusalem
Ex-Cops And Robbers
The World of Comics
When Time Was Endless

Biography/Memoir

Dual Mission
Living With Madness

REFERENCE

Resumes That Impress!
Resumes For Higher Paying Positions

Send Messages to

BestSellerPublications@gmail.com

Dedication

To everyone who has embraced life
despite not having a clue as to what it means.

Acknowledgements

A special thanks is reserved for Hillary Blackton, Donald Palmer, Jackie Seamon, Kenneth Weiss, and Margaret Smith who offered literary suggestions that influenced the author's efforts in writing this book.

"To Err is Human."
—Alexander Pope

Table of Contents

Chapter 1: In the Beginning

To look at him, you would see a short, thin, well-dressed man. Little would you know that inside was a racing mind with limitless ideas. This was the plight, the nature, the instinct of the writer, one who could create a universe, not in seven days, but rather in seven minutes.

The writer had the imagination to invent anything, to birth any character, and script any message. A writer, through forethought and revision, could perfect what a character says and does, so that the outcome would be exactly what should happen, instead of what would actually happen. And so, who was worthy of such acclaim — the almighty creator: the writer.

To be honest, it was an involuntary mode of constant reflection, reasoning, fantasizing, hypothesizing, and ruminating. His mind observed, deconstructed, and extrapolated opinions of the world that he had to dramatize through a story.

But who was this writer? Was he as ordinary as he seemed from his outward appearance? The writer's name is "Bic" Penman. It's really Barry Penman, but his friends couldn't help amusing themselves by calling him by the brand name of a popular pen. Other nicknames that didn't have as much lasting power were "Penmanship" and "Bearman," which was a hybrid of Barry and Penman. But "Bic" somehow stuck.

Barry…rather Bic, finished another long, fruitless day as an employee of a federal contractor where he was underutilized. His majestic literary talents that could rival Hemmingway were overlooked by his bureaucratic employer. Instead, he was expected to write technical manuals on computer systems. This was on a good day. For most days, he was reduced to editing, proofreading, and fact checking. During these stretches of perfunctory duties, his talents went into atrophy.

It must be premised that, for this federal contractor, Bic and his colleagues were contractually restricted to work only on assignments that were approved by their designated government points-of-contact. He could not begin new initiatives on a whim even if he saw a way to improve efficiency. Any and all actions were regulated by the government client, the Department of Transportation, which drove him crazy. Therefore, for proficient employees who completed their assignments in a timely manner, there was little to do but chat up a storm with colleagues.

Bic's office floor was staffed by about 100 employees called the Project Team. It consisted of various technical professionals: engineers, computer security personnel, analysts, developers, testers, and help desk colleagues. Unfortunately, Bic was stereotypically a reclusive loner who slinked around rather than engaged in debates over the Wizard's playoff win or recap of the latest episode of The Big Bang Theory.

Much of the staff were the twenty-something generation who interacted with each other seamlessly. But Bic already had a daughter their age and felt a little out of place at

50. His mind would occasionally entertain the idea of retirement in the not-too-distant future, which made him feel dismal in respect that he should be at the height of his success. But instead, he was relegated to writing dry technical manuals that read like this: "*From the desktop, double-click the Account Management System Application Icon. When the Home page appears, click the Account Management tab on the main menu to reveal the drop-down menu. Select the New Account option to display the New Account form.*" It could put a colicky infant to sleep.

But he couldn't up and quit. Technical Writers were royally paid. It was one of the few jobs as a writer that commanded high compensation. The job's only flaw was that the writing demands were moronic. Technical writing was the most unimaginative, straight line in Information Technology. And to an artist like Bic Penman, it was not only boring, but offensive to his sensibilities.

To get through the unbearable ennui of handling dry technical manuals, Bic managed his day with cleverly disguised diversions. He'd leave the office building and walk across the street to the café and get a coffee. The coffee was a critical prop to get through a boring day. Not only could he nurse it for a couple of hours, but it enabled him to get up from his chair every 20 minutes and warm it up in the break room. Of course, after the fifth time he "nuked it," the molecular structure of the coffee mutated into some other life form that was more bitter than he was. So, of course, that meant he must go back to the café to get a fresh cup. This ploy could repeat three times throughout the day.

The policy for lunch time clearly references the duration to be no longer than 30 minutes. This applied, apparently to all those who have read this policy and to those who blindly obeyed it. That person would not be Bic. Since the 100 employees on the 5th floor of the Transportation building took their lunch break at various times between 11:30 to 1:00, clearly the comings and goings of all these people caused enough confusion that Bic could slip away for at least an hour. Rules didn't really apply to him anyway. When he drove through a stop sign and the passenger complained, "Hey Bic, you just drove through a stop sign." He replied, "Yeah but you didn't read the fine print. It said, 'Stop if you damn well feel like it.'" So, let's say Bic was not quite a conformist. A good employee? Well maybe under the right circumstances where his mind was challenged and a lot was expected of him. But in the lackadaisical culture of federal contracting, the mind was clearly a wasteland. He was in essence in prison doing his time, waiting for retirement.

After lunch, it was back to his diversions. On a pad he calculated how much money he could save and invest each year. Then he projected just how many years it would take for his estate to be worth a million dollars. That was his magic number when he would retire and do something more meaningful with his mind and life. By packing away the money now, he could retire at 58 and start his publishing company, write more books, and maybe teach college courses.

At 5:00 pm, Bic exited the office building. The winter evening took away the daylight early. For his commute, it was another long walk through the dark streets of Washington, DC to get to the Metro. Bic slung his hand bag full of his notes over his shoulder and hoofed it across town.

Bic's way home took him through an underpass. The freight trains rumbled overhead. The pedestrian tunnel was even darker and more secluded, but it was the way he always walked. Midway through the tunnel, a figure emerged. He was a youth, but looking to be recognized. He was tall and thin, hooded and menacing. Bic knew something wasn't going to go his way, especially when two more grown men made themselves known from the darkness. Bic stopped walking. He looked over his shoulder seeing the dimming light of dusk from the tunnel's entrance. Retreat was on his mind. Before he could conjure any other plan, three more bedraggled men circled him. Bic couldn't avoid noticing the hallmarks of the clichéd thug: missing teeth; dirty, baggy clothes; scraggly facial hair. Like a pack of sewer rats, they surrounded the well-dressed professional knowing exactly what they wanted. Almost with ridiculous expectations, Bic asked, "What do you want?"

One of the older members of the circle motioned to the young thin one to assert himself. He spoke boldly, "Gimme your wallet, Mr. Park Avenue."

Just then, Bic kicked into survival mode. A swell of confidence filled his senses. He was under-employed, but none-the-less, an artistic genius. This self-awareness gave him an overpowering sense of self determination. Right or wrong, he knew he had a purpose in life: to capture it by writing novels that had not yet been written. If he had to experience the gritty underworld by getting robbed and beaten up, so be it. It would be the stuff of his next great novel.

At this critical moment, the youth got into Bic's face expecting the working man to give up his "hard" earned dollars. Before any of the gang said another word, Bic sucked in his gut and pressed out his chest in an instinctual posture of self-preservation. He then bellowed, "Do you know who I am?" The gang was silent. They were expecting Bic to cave. It looked like they would have a beat down. Hearing no response from the gang, Bic answered his own question, "I," he paused for emphasis, "am a Technical Writer." The gang members recoiled. Bic picked out a writing instrument from his pocket. "I am armed with a mechanical pencil." Bic brandished his pencil like it was a gold cross before a vampire. "If you don't let me pass unharmed, I will write you each a disparaging note!"

The gang members uniformly gasped, then cowered at the threat. The homeless man yelled out in vain, "I think he means it." Another one of the gang mumbled, "That dude's crazy." Three of the men high-tailed away, but three others stood in a stupor not knowing what to do. Then one of the hooded men cried out, "I don't believe you would do that, man." Bic lost his patience, "All right, you first." Bic wrote a note on the back of a receipt he had in his pocket, and then did the same for the other two. The three gang members squinted in the dim tunnel. One complained, "I can't read mines. His handwriting is worse than a doctor's." Then he made out the note and lost his composure, "Noooo! It says that I'm jejune." Another one bawled out, "He wrote that I have a picayune mind!" Then he started whimpering. "Take it back, please." The last one cried out, "He wrote that I'm a cliché of the underworld not worthy of fictional depiction."

Bic placed his hands behind his backside as would a scholar and strolled through the underpass leaving behind the emotionally destroyed hooligans to ponder their lost souls. Then Bic awoke from his spacy daze and realized he was still at work and that his eyes were open, locked in place waiting for the minute hand to reach 5:00 pm. His life had become so miserably stagnant that his mind had to generate excitement by creating a world of its own. He was truly a writer who created something out of nothing.

Like most writers, Bic was aloof, and, in the name of the stereotypical writer, he was lonely. His problem was that the ladies he met must always compete with his imagination of who he would like to be with. The reality of an actual person with all their shortcomings, quirks, and idiosyncrasies could never compete with the perfection he conceived.

In Bic's mind, he saw his prospective mate as a sophisticated woman with a model figure, in a tight short dress and high heels. Her midnight-black hair hung in gentle curls. She had strong facial features with well-defined cheek bones and sharp jaw line. She was a confident socialite; a writer like himself who was accomplished with volumes of work to her credit and accolades from the industry. When she walked into a room, people stopped what they were doing to watch her. Her beauty transcended all standards, even of the most powerful men — the tallest and most athletic, and the most dashing players took notice of her.

Her name? It changed with Bic's mood. Sometimes it was Rita. Other times it was Rachela. He just knew that when she, in all her beauty, walked hand-in-hand with him to a party, the other men not only would leer at his siren of a date, but also look at him with envy. "Look all you want gentlemen. Tonight, when we all go home to bed, I will be making love to a goddess." Then Bic realized that every woman he actually does meet must compete with this unrealistic fantasy. Women he met were never good enough; they never came close, because they were real.

America recently celebrated a new year: 2020. In this digital social media era, people sought romantic partners through on-line dating websites. Bic viewed hundreds of profiles dismissing one after another because of the blight of their picture or something irritatingly written in their profile. As soon as he saw the word "God" as in "I owe my inner strength to the almighty God," he discarded them faster than Jesus turned water into merlot. Frankly, if they didn't believe in evolution, they became extinct in his mind.

He was looking for his "Rita" in a pool of women. But he didn't dare jump off the diving board into this pool. It was too shallow. Some of the women had serious demands of their own. "Must open car door for me."

Bic didn't know the ultimate answers to life, like everyone else, but he knew a few things. First, he knew he liked having money more than not having money. Secondly, he knew despite the inevitable disappointments of the opposite sex, he liked wining and dining women more than staying home Saturday nights watching the Bird channel. Thirdly, he knew if you meet the first condition of having money, you would more likely achieve the second condition of being able to wine and dine the ladies. As evidence of this, he recalled a conversation he once had with a lady friend. Bic asked her innocently enough, "Do you want to marry someone rich?" He didn't expect her face to contort as she replied sourly, "No, I want to marry someone on welfare!" Point understood.

Unlike in his youth, Bic now had some assets. He could afford to entertain his dates at upscale restaurants without cringing if she ordered a glass of wine.

So, the writer was faced with writing his own profile and posting it on the DateNow website for singles. This proved to be an intimidating task even for a skilled writer. What does one say that doesn't sound trite, self-righteous, or contrived? The profiles of other members certainly do. It seemed as if every woman online loved to travel the world. Where do they get all the cash and time to roam the streets, forests, and sand dunes of earth? They all seem to be quite in touch with their feelings about relationships and what they want given the extensive length of their descriptions and blunt specifics: "Must have a magnetic smile that lights up a room." And Bic thought he was struggling to distinguish reality from fantasy. But this time it's the reality of him against women's fantasies.

Bic swiped through hundreds upon hundreds of eligible women's photos. He dismissed one after the other, sometimes stopping at the more hideous creatures out of admiration that someone so beastly would either have the guts to put themselves out there or the necessary amount of self-delusion. It was as fascinating as passing a fatal car accident. As one would wonder if anyone survived, he wondered whether these unfortunate women could actually attract another person. Some of them had reasonable attributes and interests; they just had what Bic referred to as a "general facial problem. You know the ones that have hair growth on their chins to the point where a regular shave wouldn't be good enough. No, they would need to invest in a Norelco machine to cut through that kind of facial thicket." Okay, at this point, you could agree, despite Bic's reserved nature, he has a bit of a vitriolic sense of humor. But consider what Bic was up against in contemporary American culture.

Women searched for men who were over 6 feet tall, had salaries above $100,000 a year with prestige, power, or authority. Otherwise, they had to be a bad boy riding a Harley and a body inked with tattoos. Bic didn't fit in any of those roles. A guy with a motorcycle could take his date on a thrill ride all the while she had her arms tightly wrapped around his abdomen. What was a writer going to say, "Would you like to come over to my home and watch me write a short story on a classic typewriter?" Not quite as much of an adrenalin rush.

With his thoughts swirling about, Bic wrote a basic profile emphasizing his eclectic interests in writing, art, music, road trips, museums, wining and dining, live theatre, and signed with his handle: "BicPen." His assumption was that most people responded to the picture anyway. If they were tempted with the appearance, they will respond. Although, an attractive woman may get bombarded with contacts from sex-driven guys, the profiles of men often didn't receive unsolicited mail. Men were the ones expected to initiate contact. So, Bic's profile was more of an exercise in futility.

Bic researched the inventory of profiles and compiled a number of potential women to contact. He narrowed the selection, and then it became obvious who he should try to captivate: Marisa Bookman-RabDoc. Her last name alone was a sign. Yes, Bic was a relentless empiricist who despised pseudo sciences such as astrology, phrenology, psychic readings, etc. But he was also a romantic at heart. Any two people with the last names of Penman and Bookman belong together to write their own story, a novel for the ages with eternal meaning and until "death do us part."

"So, who is Marisa Bookman," Bic mused, "and what in the world does RabDoc mean?"

First, a perusal of her profile: "Warm, witty, wise (and alliterative) woman looking for the last first date that can lead to the rest of a great life together. Looking for a man with intelligence, insight, and integrity. While I'm a reader and a thinker, I also love to hang out, listen to NPR, watch independent films, and entertain family and friends."

As enticing as her message was, it left a lot about her to learn. What did she do for a living? Does she have kids? Is she happy? Why is she single? Is she in good health, good conversationalist, and lover? Is she honest, faithful, and sexy? Is she financially responsible? Is she emotionally stable? Too many questions, and they applied to anybody Bic would meet. Could he really find love through Internet matchmaking? It was the culture of the age he lived in. At least they were able to see pictures of each other. The rest would have to unfold more conventionally through conversation and experience.

Bic clicked on Marisa's profile page and entered a text message: "Dear 'warm, witty, and wise woman.' Perhaps we could meet over a cup of coffee? Not the same cup of course. You would have your own cup, and I would drink from a different, separate cup. Otherwise, we would butt each other in the forehead trying to drink from the same cup at the same time. Sincerely memorable, mellow, and mild-mannered man. Bic"

"P.S. Your cup of coffee is my treat. I am very concerned about your forehead."

After a few email exchanges, RabDoc and BicPen agreed to meet at a local Starbucks at

1:00 pm Sunday afternoon. Bic arrived a little early to stake out the place. He didn't want to show up in a rush hyperventilating and befuddled. It felt much like a job interview. He would have to put on an air of confidence and pleasantness but not seem disingenuous. Or maybe he would let it all hang out. Who knew?

Bic, like most people who dated online, had his share of horror stories. One lady friend of his, who happened to be obese, complained that on an online date, she drove up to her date's car for their first meeting, the guy took one look at her and said, "Don't bother getting out," and drove away.

Of course in Bic's experience, he had faced some of the more routine deceptions: women who posted sensational pictures of themselves, but from 10 years ago when they were cute and hot. When he met them, their double chin and absence of a waistline came as disappointments.

Bic sat in a lounge chair, glancing at the Starbuck's entrance and assessed each patron as they entered. He thought that maybe he should prepare to take a quick picture as soon as she walked in to document the first moment he laid eyes on her, but just as quickly dropped the romantic idea, thinking she may feel that was too creepy or presumptuous. Besides it wasn't completely obvious who she was. Then a woman that appeared similar to her description, 5'7", long, brown hair came walking through the door. She had a sour expression and was way too heavy for his slender frame. Out of obligation, he approached her, "Are you Marisa?" The woman dismissed him and walked past. He exhaled in complete relief despite the cold rejection. Then an attractive forty-something woman entered and took a cursory look around. She wore a fashionable leather jacket and shoulder length hair with gentle curls. She approached him, "Bic?" "Yeah," he replied. "Marisa?" "How are you? I thought someone else was you at first," she admitted. "Me too." They chuckled and embraced with a reassuring quick hug. "I'm glad you're you," Bic said. "Thanks. I like being me," she replied.

Bic offered to buy her a coffee or tea and went to the barista for his order while Marisa found a vacant table free of crumbs. He returned with the coffee. "See, I told you Marisa. Your own cup."

"That's what attracted me to you. Your sense of humor."

"Oh, I thought it was my 5'6" stature," he quipped.

She smiled. "What drew you to my profile?" she inquired. He explained that he was fishing for someone who would respond to his brand of humor. And Marisa bit the worm off Bic's lure. For all of Bic's wisdom and insight into human nature, foremost he didn't take many things seriously. He exploited every opportunity to make a joke. A reasonable gesture on a first date. Or maybe he was always a reasonable jester. Who knew?

Bic noticed that he was taller than Marisa. Hmm. An idea popped into his head. "Marisa, on your profile, you indicated that you were 5'7"."

"Yeah," she said innocently enough.

Bic replied, "But I'm taller than you and I'm only 5'6"." She appeared puzzled. "Stand up," he said, "and slip off your high-heels." She did. He turned her back to his back first to compare heights, but really to glance his buttocks against hers in a premature effort to experience intimacy. He slid his hand over his head and down over hers. "Yep, you completely misrepresented yourself. You're not 5'7," unless you are counting your high heels as an extension of your feet. You're 5'4" at best."

"Well would you rather that I be 5'7" and taller than you? How would you feel then, Bic?" she defended and challenged, revealing a feistiness that he respected.

"If I thought you were really too tall for me, I would have come prepared. I would have brought a step stool. You would just have had to walk slowly next to me so that I could keep moving it forward while we walked."

She did her best not to roll her eyes. "You know I usually don't date men at Starbucks. Consider yourself lucky," she said.

"Well I usually don't date men at Starbucks either, so consider YOURself lucky," was his riposte.

"Be serious for a moment. Don't you realize if we ever got seriously involved, every time we go to a dinner party and people ask, 'So how did you guys meet?' we will have to say we met through a dating website, and our first date was at Starbucks?"

"Yeah, well, that will be the same story everyone else in our generation will be telling too. That's the age we live in," Bic said reflectively.

Marisa replied, "Yeah, but it's not as romantic as saying we met while relaxing on the Venetian canals when our gondolas collided." She smiled almost imperceptibly.

"Well…it could be," Bic declared. "We could just make up a romantic story and go with it. Who would know any differently?"

She smirked at him. "You're bad."

"I am. I am a true bad boy, my dear. I drive through stop signs. I once got a tattoo. Of course it was water soluble, so you can't see it anymore. But at least you know I bathe. And yes, I do have a dark side."

"You are a joker, Bic. How did you get that name anyway? And your handle, BicPen, what's that mean?"

"It's just a nickname. Barry is my real name. My last name is Penman and I'm a writer. So my friends call be Bic. What does your on-line handle mean, RabDoc?"

She explained, "I completed rabbinical school and I'm a psychologist, as in Rabbi and Doctor."

"A female rabbi? Progressive!" he said supportively, though also concealing his contempt for organized religion. He then joked, "We didn't even say a blessing for the coffee."

She felt at ease in the presence of a lantzman. To show off her deftness, she obliged, "*Barukh attah Adonai, Eloheinu melekh haolam, shehakol niyah bidvaro.*" Marisa smiled as she finished blessing the coffee in ancient Hebrew.

Bic's brows rose and his lids relaxed in a sign of disengagement, "I attended Hebrew school three times a week for six years. After all that, I could only memorize one prayer."

"Not a scholar huh!" Marisa feigned empathy, but still smitten with Bic's carefree openness, a quality she found endearing.

"I was ADHD growing up." Bic volunteered, "Academics were a challenge. The teachers all hated me because I kept drawing outside the lines."

"A lot of my patients have Attention Deficit Hyperactive Disorder."

Bic replied, "So shouldn't we be having this date on a couch or something? I don't have to pass a Rorschach test, do I?" he asked matter-of-factly.

She smiled, "No couch. So long as you don't make me pass a grammar test."

"Deal," Bic agreed and opened up the conversation. "So, what's a stable-minded psychologist doing on the dating scene dealing with all the single sociopaths?"

"I have met some interesting characters," Marisa replied, "but no connections. I'm looking for a committed life together, to share a life with someone who I can grow old with. So many men on websites just want to hook up for sex. So, tell me something about your past relationships. Were you ever married?"

Bic dragged his will to retell the story he had told many times over the years, "Yeah sure, my ex left me in 2001. When I came home, she was gone. I celebrated by throwing a party. But it's been 19 years as a bachelor. So most of the helium balloons have dropped to the floor and the party members have gone home. Now I'm stepping on too many fallen balloons and can say I may be ready to share a life with someone. So those are some reflective shards from the shattered mirror of my past life."

"Sharp words. After my breakup, I too was floating party balloons — actually, more like the Bullwinkle-float size ones, when my marriage ended in 2003. It was way too long in coming. What are you doing for the long holiday weekend?" she asked.

"What does an unhitched bachelor do on such a long weekend? He throws a pretend party for all of his imaginary friends. That's good news and bad news," he said nonchalantly. "First the bad news: I'm throwing imaginary parties. The good news: while I'm at them, I really enjoy myself." Marisa's face resisted a smile. Then Bic pondered a moment and inquired, "You don't think there is anything inherently contradictory in being a rabbi and a doctor?"

Marisa shrugged slightly and matter-of-factly stated, "Science and religion don't contradict each other." Then said bluntly, "One's the pursuit of knowledge; the other is the acknowledgment of the unknown, a surrender to powers beyond our understanding and comprehension?"

Bic tossed up his fingers flippantly, "Look, I'm just a particles and probability man. No super being in the heavens for me."

"Then how do you explain reality, where your so called particles and probability come from? How did nothing become something?"

"The same could be said of God." Bic stated, then countered, "Okay, let's say you buy into the whole idea of the Higher Power." Bic spoke candidly in opposition, asking rhetorically, "So where is he when good men and women die, get harmed, or suffer? Where was he during all the genocides, tragic accidents, and natural disasters throughout history? Why don't those people's prayers get answered?"

Not fazed by his logic, Marisa explained her paradigm, "You don't seem to grasp the idea of faith. Spirituality is not something subject to verifiable observation. Faith is the acknowledgement of the unknown and the unknowable. The rituals are expressions of that respect."

Feeling a mission to uncover Bic's spiritual identity, Marisa asked, "I don't understand how you can call yourself Jewish and not believe in God."

Bic collected his thoughts, "I would answer you by saying that I don't see Judaism strictly as a religion. I see it more as a culture and race. I am genetically Jewish because my parents and other ancestors were Jewish. I am culturally Jewish because I share and am familiar with the history of the Jews, the Hebrew language, customs and shared values such as education, financial responsibility, and good will towards others. I eat bagels, with lox!"

Marisa's eyebrows rose, "So you think that remembering a single prayer after six years of Hebrew school makes you Jewish? You think you are Jewish by default without an invested practice and commitment to the customs and rituals? Without a trace of real faith? If you have no faith, how can you possibly consider yourself at all a member of the chosen people?"

Bic smirked knowingly, "Let me ask you something. Who would you rather I be? A devout, orthodox Jew who performs all of the religious rituals, but who has committed terrible sins, like murder, or me, an atheist who has never harmed anyone?"

Marisa rebutted, "That's not fair; a killer is not really someone living the code of the scripture."

"But that's reality," he said. "Everyone exercises bad judgment from time to time or commits a sin. And who says a religious person lives without sin? And who says a non-religious person can't lead an exemplary life? The label by which you call yourself doesn't determine your honorability; your decisions and behavior do."

"So, you simply don't believe in a higher power?" Marisa opened her palms. "Then how do you explain all of this, the world, reality?" she spread out her arms.

A silence came between the two singles as they looked deeply into each other's eyes, like they were mirrors facing each other, seeing infinity. Bic broke the silence and attempted to bridge their divide. "I do admit though that there is no real contradiction between science and religion. They are two different paradigms. I just think organized religion assumes a role that exceeds the notion of faith. Religious leaders shun diversity, evolution in thought, and dissent. Established religions promote the idea that behavior and attitudes are fixed and absolute without change."

Marisa looked around the café, then stirred her coffee again. She regained her composure, "Now you are just being ridiculous. You don't have all of the answers."

"Okay," Bic said, "but I don't pretend to either. I seek answers where answers are possible. I'm here on this earth temporarily, and all I want to do is participate in it. I want to contribute by writing books."

Marisa posed her own questions to Bic, "But if life is temporary as you say. Why bother, what's driving you?

He looked into her confused eyes and a calmness took over. She returned a direct look into his eyes and, despite the clash in views, Marisa was enraptured.

The impasse of their perceptions and values could not be any greater, yet the two singles remained seated across from each other with no less respect for each other, but rather warmed with an intense intrigue. They came from opposing views yet captivated each other's attention with an appreciation of each other's convictions. Their passionate commitment to their values intensified their attraction, but could it last for a promising future?

Jimmy, the baristo, wiped the counter with a wet towel and glanced over the lobby. In his early twenties, he stood tall and thin, his head thick with tossed hair and Elvis-like sideburns. A gold ring pierced his nostril, and a dreamy group of skulls tattooed his neck. He looked over to one of the lounge chairs and saw an obese, homeless man sound asleep. Jimmy knew this "patron" as "Crazy Carl" whose convex stomach gently rose and fell with each rumbling snore. Crazy Carl was as settled as a cigarette butt nestled in an ashtray as he remained in a smoldering slumber.

Another clerk, Rebecca, who was a stocky, 16-year-old with a boyish face and sporting a butch haircut buzzed nearly to her scalp, asked Jimmy, "Hey, should I wake up that man over there?"

Jimmy shrugged, "I don't like doing that. That's "Crazy Carl." Ya never know how these guys are gonna be like, ya know? Word on the street says, he's killed people with his bare hands as a grunt during Vietnam."

"What's that?" the issue eluding her limited youth.

"The United States was in a war in a country called Vietnam for about 10 years during the 1960s and 1970s. It didn't go so well. A lot of the soldiers came home a little whacked out. And he's one of those nut jobs. Know what I mean?"

"Not really. Do you mean he's dangerous?" she inquired. "What about the policy?" Rebecca raised the question about the policy that patrons cannot sleep in the shop.

"Hey, I'm not gunna get my head blown off just because of corporate." Then Jimmy said, "You can wake him if you want. I don't care."

"Well, if you're too much of a wuss, I will."

"Wait a minute!" Jimmy interrupted. "I'll tell you what. See this strange couple in the middle? With the guy talking his head off?"

"Yeah, so?"

"So. They're obviously on their first date. I'll bet you that Crazy Carl wakes up before their date ends?"

Rebecca looked over to Crazy Carl and then over to Bic and Marisa. "Sleepy over there is pretty far gone. I think I hear him snoring. Are you sure you want to lose?"

"I'm not going to lose. If you've been hearing this guy talk. I don't even think he breathes when he talks."

"What do I get if I win?

"Loser takes on the late shift Friday night."

"Deal. So, what's going on so far?" she asked.

"Well, the guy is like completely taking over the conversation, talking like he knows everything about everything. See how he's sitting like he owns the world, or something."

"What about the woman?"

"She's all into him for some weird reason. I don't get it myself. She's still kind of hot for a woman her age. What's she see in him? She just kind of sits there all hypnotized or something. I don't know if they're arguing or what?"

Bic looked into Marisa's eyes. His look caressed her face and followed the edge of her defined cheek bones. Then suddenly, Marisa reacted to Bic. "All right, all right, I give up," Marisa said exasperated. "We're different. Let's change the subject. Tell me about your history of relationships. You still have faith in relationships, don't you? What do you want out of woman? What do you expect?"

It doesn't take long for Bic to rattle off a description based on his many past experiences with on-line dates that have gone sour. "One that doesn't ask me how much my 401k is worth on the first date."

"Someone actually asked you that?" Marisa's eyes widened in disbelief.

Bic nodded and continued, "I'm also done with women who have manic depression, personality disorders, or who are complainers, drama queens, or cheaters…the list is quite long actually. Let's just say someone sane. Yeah, I'll go with sanity."

"Well you know, no one's perfect."

Bic scooted his behind to the edge of the chair and extended his legs in a relaxed manner that would be more appropriate in his own living room, then clarified, "I don't think my criterion of sanity raises the bar too high. I'm looking for someone who doesn't create their own crises out of thin air." Bic elaborated, "I dated a woman once who had two kids. She was pulled over by the cops and given a sobriety test, which she failed. As a result, her driver's license was revoked for 90 days. On the first day of her suspension, she drives her kids 120 miles to King's Dominion in Virginia because she said she didn't want to break her promise to them. I'm done with yahoos like that."

Marisa probed, "Bic, do you have some sort of derision towards the female gender?"

"No," he denied emphatically. "I have a sort of derision towards stupid people. I just happen to date women, so that's where my frustration lies. If I were dating men, I'm sure I would have plenty of stupid men anecdotes." Bic placed his hands behind his head confidently and said, "I'm sure your history with men have had disappointments."

"Sure. Of course," she admitted. "Who hasn't struggled in a relationship? My former husband didn't spend any time at home or with the kids. And I got sick of it. But when he came home drunk and hit me. That was it. I took the kids and walked out. In my practice, I hear firsthand from women who report domestic abuse from their husbands or boyfriends. It's all too common."

"No doubt," Bic said, "There are plenty of differences between the genders, but that doesn't seem to stop the drive to have a complementary mate. It's the idea of sharing a life together."

Encouraged by this glint of optimism, Marisa asked the red flag question, "Do you want to get married?"

Seeing another opportunity to exploit her phraseology, Bic asked, "Aren't you supposed to get down on one knee when you propose?"

"Ha, Ha," she mustered. "In general."

"I don't see the point in it at our age. You're 46 and I'm 50. We aren't going to start a new family. What is the point of marriage anyway? It's really nothing more than a symbolic status that also happens to be legally binding, which causes all sorts of bureaucracy and financial risks for both parties if things don't work out."

"You're quite the optimist!" She laughed mockingly.

"It's reality sweetheart," he replied in earnest. "We and just about everyone else have had at least one failed marriage and a host of failed relationships. When the average divorce rate is 50%, why wouldn't I be pessimistic about the odds of a successful union? Especially since most of the other 50% who remain married aren't necessarily in bliss, and perhaps wish they could part. So, my opinion is, if two people really love each other, they will stay with each other despite not having a legally binding contract. And if it goes bad, they just split without the hassle of divorce."

Marisa crinkled her brow dismissively, "That's certainly not attractive to me. If a man wants me, he has to marry me. It's a matter of trust and security. I want to know that it will be forever."

Bic returned a look of sincerity, "But marriage isn't forever. It lasts as long as the two people agree to maintain it. Which could be said for any other type of relationship. Therefore, a marriage is nothing more than a legality that is designed to prevent people from easily breaking up. But if a party is unhappy, he or she will end it anyway and experience all of the unpleasant actions necessary for divorce. Then there is the issue of assets. I worked my whole life to save what I have. And I would like to bequeath any leftovers to my daughter when I die. Why should my new bride be the beneficiary of my estate and leave it up to her to look after my daughter's interests?"

"Daughter? How old?"

"Ruti will be 20 this Memorial Day."

"Do you have a good relationship with Ruti?"

"The best. And I wouldn't want her to deal with a bunch of legalities if I should part early."

"You could always get a will or trust or something," she offered.

Bic commented, "Yeah, more bureaucracy that could be challenged in court. The bottom line is that marriage is more ritual. It's more status to tell the world you are civilized and respectable. Now how does saying 'I do' make someone who doesn't have respectability into a person who is respectable?"

She defended, "Marriage is a great responsibility. To take care of a family. Taking a passage from your stockpile of self-made clichés, it's a 'societal agreement on how to live.'"

Bic refuted, "But the status of 'married' doesn't cause anyone to be better than they are. Hence, an irresponsible person will be irresponsible in a marriage. Character, competence, and habits don't change upon the utterance of a vow. The respectability is just another illusion, a societal conditioning."

"You like pontificating on your soap box, don't you? Some people take it seriously and rise to the challenge. Without a commitment like marriage, it's far too easy to up and leave without careful consideration. Marriage prevents careless surrender during the inevitable ebbs and flows of a serious relationship."

"Hey, I call them like I see them. People just accept what society and their parents tell them. Parents tell them that they should pray to God to ensure a healthy outcome, yet outcome is the result of physics. Parents say 'eat the crust of your bread; it's good for you.' And so throughout childhood and adulthood, you accept this as gospel, only to one day realize and question, why is the crust good for you? What is crust anyway, other than the burnt side of the bread? So why is something that is cooked longer any better for you than the non-burned part of the bread? The truth is the crust is no better or worse for you than the rest of the bread. There's no nutritional difference," Bic said.

Hardly inhaling for air, Bic continued heaping on to his argument, "You, Marisa, should know something about conditioning, being a psychologist. Religion and marriage are both by-products of conditioning. People accept these institutions because they create an illusion of structure in their lives and when society tells you this is the way it is, most people respond in a predictably obedient Pavlovian way."

"You don't believe in religion or marriage; what do you believe in, Bic? What is your purpose in life? Who is Bic Penman? Tell me his story," she inquired with uncertain expectations.

Just then Crazy Carl stirred. His eyes remained closed yet his hand responded to an itch on his belly, which he scratched for a long moment. His big belly rolled to the side and a sharp snore threatened to end the bet between the baristas. But he resumed a gentle, unconscious-like slumber.

Rebecca said, "I'm not sure I'm cool with the bet."

"Hey a bet's a bet. You can't go back on your word," Jimmy said excitedly.

"Okay, okay, How about double the stakes, but we tweak the bet a little," Rebecca negotiated.

"I'm listening." Jimmy flipped an empty 16-ounce paper cup into the air. It summersaulted a few times and landed upright back into his grasp as a statement of his spirited confidence.

"Let's say, if they agree to a second date. I win. If not, you win."

"Oh, you are so on, Rebecca. This guy doesn't have a chance to get it on with this gal. Be prepared to wash some dishes this Friday night while I'm at the Death By Design concert."

"Why are you so confident they won't find each other?"

"Trust me I know. I've been working here a while. These old guys don't know how to get it on with others. You got to meet people, you know, at a party or something, where you can get high from a grab-bag of party drugs and see who you wake up with the next morning."

Rebecca pinched her lips and shook her head. "No. They're too old for that. To them, a drink at a café is a wild night out. You'll see. The guy's got gray roots in his hair. And the woman dresses too young for her age, like she's hanging on to her thirties for dear life, but she's long passed her thirties. Women can tell these

things. You don't see it, but they're having the
time of their lives."

"Who am I?" Bic asked. "I am the summation of every insight worth having and every memory worth remembering. I'm all about writing the insights of life," he stated factually.

"Yeah, okay, insights," she echoed. "Which insights are you talking about? The God doesn't exist insight, or the marriage will never last insight? Most people call that fear of commitment, but let's hear your," she air quoted, "insights."

Bic inhaled, then said, "I mean anything that I observe or notice, that strikes me as extreme, odd, unique, contradictory, ironic, or helps reveal the causes and circumstances that make people feel happy, sad, etc." Bic leaned in closer, and with an intensity to his tone, said, "I want to tap into the full gamut of human emotion and intellect: to depict experiences that most people don't have, to expand their understanding of human nature and reality. And I want to do it by stringing together words that titillate the mind and touch the soul. Language and insight, ideas and imagination are cornerstones of humanity. And I want to bottle it up and save it for the ages."

Marisa responded, "The psychologist in me is picking up on a theme here. So, in other words, you want to live forever through story telling?"

"In a way," Bic got closer to agreeing with his date. "Don't you want to put your stamp on society and leave an indication that you were alive and did something, rather than just leaving an epitaph?" Bic posed to her.

"So, the atheist shows signs of a spiritual streak," Marisa laughed loudly then accused, "You're a closet Christian, aren't you? Don't you think this is reminiscent of the religious belief system of life after death? You're just seeking immortality through words." Thinking she has finally made him eat his words, Marisa awaited his defensive response.

But to her incredulity, Bic was unfazed and said with slow enunciation, "My dear. That is exactly what it is."

"I thought you were an atheist or a pretend Jew or something to that effect?" she mocked.

"I am. I am an atheist/Jew," he confirmed. "My imprint on society by writing books is the atheist's way of achieving immortality. However, it's a real obtainable action and goal. Not a delusionary one of an invisible deity that grants entry into Heaven or banishes us to Hell."

Marisa dismissed his thought, "That's not even Judaic. Besides, if you don't believe in your soul continuing after death, then why would you care about a legacy at all? You'll be dead." she declared.

"Exactly!" he said emphatically. "That's because I'm doing this not strictly for myself, but rather for my descendants, for generations of the future. My legacy is just satisfaction for me while I'm living. When I'm dead, you are right, I will no longer care, because I won't exist. Caring about what happens after death is truly a sport for the living, a challenge to the imagination. A challenge to the sober reality of eternal nothingness and one's ability to accept it. A legacy is an atheist's version of believing in the afterlife. The participation in society, the struggle for independence, and self-expression gives us purpose and meaning, where ultimately there is none. So let me ask you something, Marisa. Why help people defer their responsibilities to an imaginary being?"

"But don't you see, Bic? I help people deal with their lives now in part by helping them with both their emotional issues and their spirituality. To me, the issues are inseparable. I listen to them, advise them, challenge them to better themselves and adapt to societal norms that have enabled people to live harmoniously for thousands of years."

"Hey, whatever floats your boat," Bic acquiesced. "So you throw out life preservers to other people who are swallowing too much sea water. Good for you and them. I'm more concerned with the question, if you're competent, what are you going to do with that ability?" he said.

"Maybe you are biased because you internalize self-pity."

"I don't pity anything about myself. I've had many low points throughout my life, but I wouldn't relinquish them for anything. I treasure my low points as experiences of life. I need to experience pain and suffering to know what it is and work my way through it. Look, much of suffering is relative to how one perceives it and processes it. Someone can hang on to hate forever, always bothered at each recurring memory of a past wrong. I reflect at past disappointments and say they didn't keep me down. I found a way to get passed them and move on. I don't forget, I just understand them," Bic explained.

Now it's Marisa who seized opportunity to poke through to the core issues. She probed for concreteness. "Okay Bic, let's hear a real-life example of such a situation!"

"Yeah sure, to put some context to what I'm saying. Take for example when I was eleven years old. I had this terribly incompetent teacher who I despised. His name was Stuart Z. Topper. Even though it was forty years ago, the memories are as vivid as the day he and I irritated the heck out of each other. At the time, I had undiagnosed and untreated Attention Deficit Hyperactive Disorder, so paying attention in class — especially the task of reading — was difficult for me. Yet he told my mother that I was on level. I had him as a reading teacher for two years in the fifth and sixth grades, but when I entered the seventh grade I tested two years behind my peers."

Having been a therapist of children who suffered from severe physical and emotional abuse, Marisa was not impressed with Bic's issue. "And this proves what? That you had a little set-back when you were a kid? Who hasn't had them?" She continued, "Look, I've counseled kids whose parents extinguished lit cigarettes on their skin, and you whine about reading?"

"Not exactly, Marisa. My lack of attention and poor education caused chronic anxiety and depression, low self-esteem, and poor academics for years. Yet the constant failings over the years challenged me to turn it around and prove I could do it. By the time I entered college I was committed to doing my best and shined here and there. And look at me now, a writer and author. My natural talents matured nonetheless."

Marisa reflected a moment. She realized the discussion was all about him thus far. She decided to make a declaration of her own. "That's why it's so important to have a good support system. Like a relationship, a spouse who can help you through the tough times and be your greatest advocate."

"But as you know Marisa, even a spouse who declares their love can one day turn on a dime and mistreat you in the worst way. People aren't perfect."

"Well, in a relationship, I want everything to be just as I expect it. If I don't get what I want I leave."

Bic pounced on her, "Then you suffer the same affliction as most — battling the expectation of perfection while experiencing the reality of anything but perfection."

Marisa reassured Bic, "Look, I'll be the first to recognize the vast array of people with problems and imperfections. I deal with real people every day. They are flawed people who aren't scripted like TV characters or photoshopped magazine models. They don't really like to smile all the time. They have insecurities, obsessions, quirks, bad habits, not to mention limited bank accounts, asymmetrical faces, short statures, pot bellies, and unkempt bedrooms. I listen to all this during therapy sessions." Marisa finally gets to the point that when someone who is fairly in the ballpark crosses our path, we don't take advantage and approach them, or let them into our worlds. We don't even bother exploring the possibility of a match. We're too busy seeing the one percent of the population blessed with a great physique, stunning facial features, and complete immersion in designer clothing. The others are dismissed. "They are what I call the invisibles. They are all around us, but aren't seen. It's sad because once you get to know someone, their values, their soul, their outward appearance appears ingratiating no matter what they look like."

Bic listened to Marisa's commentary until she petered out, then sensed an opportunity to test her own convictions and asked, "So, you don't mind dating someone ugly?"

Just then a short, wide man entered the Starbuck's lobby. He wore a baseball cap and looked down to avoid eye contact and to conceal his whiskered face. With his hands deep in his pockets, he scanned the lobby. He saw a senior woman seated in a lounge chair, intensely focused on her lap. Her eyes squinted into the shape of the very tiny beads she was threading. She was in a world of her own, solitary, but immersed in the Starbuck's community. Crazy Carl continued to slumber, absent from the ongoings of the café. Bic and Marisa continued their bantering and intellectual ponderings that rose above any sensible first date conversation.

The short, disheveled man approached the bar counter. Rebecca, the barista, sensed an issue with the strange man, but nevertheless asked the obligatory, "How may I help you sir?" She expected him to string a medley of words that in their full relationship equaled a single, coherent drink on the menu. Instead, he mumbled, "Gimme your cash."

Rebecca appeared startled and looked to the side seeking Jimmy, but he was in the back room stocking something. She didn't know what to do. She felt an odd mixture of fear of this robber, for the patrons, for her own life, and fear of corporate if she gave in. She just couldn't give a man the money in the register, could she? She was stunned and in a psychological state of paralysis. Was it worth fighting? Hell, she didn't own the company. It was not her money. Besides getting hurt or someone else getting hurt was worse than getting ripped off. The moment of confusion ended with a sobering clarity — the worldwide, publicly traded champion of the coffee bean can afford the loss of a hundred bucks. Her senses came back to her, she snorted outward. "Go ahead, buddy. Take what's in there."

"Open it," he mumbled.

She did and he reached over and grabbed the cash. He turned around. Crazy Carl remained in a slumber. The old lady seated on the far end of the store was focused on her beads, the most important thing in her life. She didn't appear like she would have any money on her anyway, he thought. Then he set his sights on Bic and Marisa: two adults in the prime of their lives, at the highest point of their earning potential. Their wallets were probably full of credit cards and cash. He approached their table as Bic and Marisa verbally dueled.

"I never said that." Marisa seemed to back pedal. "What about you? Would you give someone not so good looking a chance?"

"No. I doubt it. I suffer from the same vanity as everybody else. The way I see it is that yes, ugly people are somewhat the same as beautiful people. They all have good points and flaws." The short man stared at Bic and caught his attention. Bic looked up to him, but continued his thoughts to Marissa, "So I figure, if I have to adapt to someone's flaws, I might as well have some eye candy along the way. Right? In other words, an obese woman may be unfairly ignored, but guess what, if for some unusual inexplicable reason I decided to date such a woman, I would still have to deal with her menstrual cycles, mood swings, insecurities, nagging, and all the other things that are inherent in any relationship. Therefore, I might as well focus on women who are good looking. That way, when I engage in a bitter argument with my date, I'll be titillated by her beauty even during the heat of battle."

Marisa leaned back, folded her arms, and said, "That must be the shallowest thing anyone has ever said to me."

The robber started to get anxious. He looked furtively every which way trying not to become frantic. He had a bit of cash already. He didn't want to get caught but sensed Bic had more for him. Still trying to be inconspicuous, the robber mumbled something to Bic, but Bic just waved him away and said "beat it dude. I'm in the middle of a conversation." Bic then returned his attention to Marisa and responded with a devilish smirk, "I'm not denying it's shallow. I'm just impressing upon you the truth my dear. Any relationship is a struggle. As soon as the honeymoon ends, each partner is wishing he or she were with someone else. Someone better. Greener pastures is the habitual lure of the imagined perfection that just isn't reality."

The short man didn't know what to do. He felt the pressure of the cops coming. He attempted again, "Hey man. I'm talkin' to you," he said to Bic.

Bic turned to him, "Hey dude. You're interrupting. I'm talkin' here. Unless you have some insight into the issue of the imagined state of perfection in contrast to the flawed state of reality, take a freak'n hike."

"You don't understand, man, I want…"

Bic turned to him impatiently. "Who are you? Napoleon's little brother? Will you get the hell away from us, bud?" Oblivious to the potential danger, Bic's abrasiveness successfully warded off the robbery with unintentional bravado.

Marisa was taken aback at the exchange and interjected, "Be civil Bic. He probably just wanted to borrow a chair or something."

Bic looked at the empty chair next to him and then looked at Marisa seriously, and quipped, "But this is my favorite chair, Marisa."

Marisa rolled her eyes equally oblivious, then pressed him, "Okay so let's say you see a woman who meets your stringent criteria of having looks that don't offend the senses. What do you do next, just ogle at her taut behind?"

The short man looked confused. He saw a young woman seated in a chair engrossed in her i-phone also oblivious that he had just robbed the café. He decided it was too risky to hang around any longer and scurried out of the café lobby.

"And that brings up a related issue. What has your relationship background been like? Do you just approach strange women and hit on them for a quick hook up?"

"No actually I'm like Captain America who emerged from decades in a frozen state to awaken in a new era."

Superheroes always seemed to find relevance in a man's way of thinking, which should have been no surprise to Marisa, but nonetheless the reference threw her. Dumbfounded with who or why this superhero is at all pertinent she said, "Explain, I'm not a Captain America aficionado. He's the one with the mask, right?"

Disappointed in her lack of knowledge of such an icon, he couldn't help but try to contain his contempt for her lack of familiarity with the famed character and said dryly, "Yeah Marissa." Then he said emphatically, "They all have masks!" Then he explained more matter-of-factly, "He's the one with the shield. This is what I mean to say. I was married for about five years and divorced in 2001. Soon after I was diagnosed with Tourette's Syndrome."

"This is getting interesting," Marisa said. "I don't have a clue as to where this is going with the whole shield thing, but I have a patient with Tourette's. He yells profanity."

"Yeah, well I have a different brand. For most people I have to explain that Tourette's is a neurological disorder characterized by involuntary movements. I don't usually get into the other half dozen subsystems. Thankfully I don't bark like a dog or yell inappropriate words uncontrollably. I only do that voluntarily."

"Well, you are more than welcome to talk it out with me. That's what I do best. But I haven't seen you tic," she said.

"I have my good days and not so good. I have a variety of classic moves. Usually my arm muscles just suddenly tense and my hand will abruptly jerk up. My whole body, including my lungs, get jarred causing me to let out a mild grunt. It's like someone suddenly pushes you on your back without any warning. You would lose your balance, but not necessarily fall. Other times, my arm will thrust in the air with my hand in a fist. I call that tic "Black Power" like the gestures African American athletes made on the podium at the 1968 Olympics in Mexico. One time I was in a meeting and my hand waved in the air. The leader of the meeting looked distracted the first time I did it; the second time, she asked me if there were flies in the office room. She thought I was waving away a fly," he snorted inward.

Marisa looked puzzled on too many levels, but finally asked pointedly, "And this relates to relationships, how? And after you explain that, you're going to have to explain how Captain America fits into all this."

"I'm getting to it. So ever since I was diagnosed with this condition, I've been taking psychotropic pharmaceuticals. As you probably know, there's no cure for Tourette's. There are just drugs that mitigate the symptoms and add a few unwanted side-effects. One of which is a reduction in libido. So while taking these pills for about 10 years, my sex drive was so muted that I frankly was not interested in either carnal pleasure or a relationship of any kind. I call them my frozen years. But recently, the psychiatrist who prescribed my medication, retired. So I went to a different doctor; she decided to prescribe a different medication. Voila, it didn't have the same side effects, and I came back to life, like Captain America defrosted from a frozen state within an iceberg after many decades."

"That's depressing, Captain."

"Actually, the hiatus kept me out of trouble, not getting into an unwanted pregnancy or STD."

"So, Bic, what was the medical wonder drug that defrosted your libido?"

"I went through Zyprexa, Sasaphris, Wellbutrin, Risperadone, Latuda, and now Vraylar. It's a new generation drug."

Marisa felt like sharing a bit of common ground and admitted, "I guess it's only fair that I tell you that I take Xanax for anxiety and depression."

"Not surprised," Bic said. "We live in a medicated society today. Everybody's got something. Everybody's chemical composition deviates from the ideal, the state of optimal performance. At least our notion of that."

Marisa sensed some opposition to treatment. She asked "Would you rather live without treatment, and let your condition dominate your daily life?"

"I wouldn't, and I couldn't," Bic quickly said. "I'm dependent on these meds. I wouldn't be able to function without them."

Marisa is reminded of a literary reference, "Looks like Aldous Huxley's message in *Brave New World* that society is headed to a drug-induced dependency for happiness was more of an exaggeration. People don't depend on drugs for happiness; prescribed drugs enable people to overcome an otherwise debilitated state. And the side effects make us anything but artificially happy."

Jimmy returned from the back storage area. He looked at Rebecca and sensed something wrong. "Did I win the bet?" he asked.

She leaned closer to him, "We just got robbed." Jimmy's eyebrows rose in surprise. "Are you okay? What happened? I was just putting some paper goods away.

"It's not your fault Jimmy."

"How much did he get?"

"Just about $100."

"Oh. That's no big deal. It's just we have to report it. That's all."

"I've already called it in to security. They'll be here in a little while to take my statement."

"Did he rob any of the patrons?"

"Na, he looked like he wanted to, but they're all in their own world and didn't notice anything."

"Not even the two in the middle? The dude who's right there?"

"He was the most unaware of them all, even more than Crazy Carl who's still snoring."

Jimmy half smiled at the reference. "So, my chance of winning the bet is looking pretty good?"

"Remember Jimmy, we changed the bet, it doesn't matter if their conversation lasts longer than sleepy head over there slumbers. The bet is whether the guy gets another date with Ms. Hotty."

"I know Rebecca. I'm not welching."

Marisa saw an opening to delve more into Bic's values and positions on issues close to her profession as a psychologist. She asked him, "So you're liberal on manipulating your physiological chemistry?"

Feeling misunderstood, Bic said sarcastically, "Well I wouldn't rely on prayer, and I'll go farther than that. I think there's no ethical limitation for the scientific community to seek out ways to improve DNA. On the horizon already is the possibility to improve on the cognitive and physical functions of the human species."

Sensing Bic had gone overboard, she asked him, "So you support medical experimentation on the human race? Nazis tried that." She almost couldn't contain herself waiting to see how he would respond after being compared to Nazis.

But Bic is a master of capitalizing on the shock value of the ugly truth, even though few would phrase it with such bluntness. "The Nazis' goals for a perfected society weren't misguided; it was their notion of what constituted perfection that was their problem. Their assumption that the Aryans constituted perfection and no one else was worthy was their downfall. Besides humans have been improving on themselves ever since the dawn of humanity. Look, the first time someone picked up a stick and used it as a cane, they were enhancing human functionality. We're just more sophisticated now with implants, prosthetics, exoskeletons, etc. It's just a matter of time before the manipulation of genes and DNA will result in designer limbs and such. If scientists can make a glow-in-the-dark cat, it's just a matter of time before some person will be born with a tail or wings, five eyes or two hearts."

Marisa felt deflated at Bic's enthusiasm for the hypothetical eugenics that may be more than a hundred years into the future. Instead, she decided to bring the conversation of values back to the present day. She thought of the most divisive issue she could and put him to the test. She asked him, "Where do you stand on abortion? Pro Choice or Pro-Life?"

Without hesitation, Bic pounced on the issue and blurted out, "Both!" A moment of silence settled the tempo, but before Marisa had a chance to ask Bic to explain the apparent contradiction of his answer, he volunteered, "I am for a woman's right to an abortion, but also recognize the pro-life position that life begins at fertilization."

"I don't understand," she said, "So how do you reconcile the right for life at conception and a woman's right for abortion?"

"Easy. I acknowledge that an abortion kills an innocent life, but that society is okay with that."

Marisa interjected, "Okay. That was way too easy for you to answer. Elaborate and justify, please."

"Sure," Bic said. "See, rights are fictitious powers bestowed upon an individual by a made-up body of authorities. The lawmakers are no authorities on any matter other than what society accepts as a consensus. Therefore, nobody really has rights other than what society agrees to. Nobody has the right to live other than if those in power agree that it should be so. So, our laws are a byproduct of consensus, not divine Truth."

Bic exhaled, sipped his coffee, took in Marisa's attention, then continued his rebuttal: "Abortions kill innocent human beings, even if those human beings are at the start of their development. It's just that most people — of decision-making ability — value the child bearer more than the future unfolding life of an embryo. Society values the tax savings of not having to imprison thugs who grew up from uncaring or incapable mothers who didn't want the pregnancy in the first place. It's that simple," Bic said emphatically.

Marisa tried to keep up with Bic's unusual argument. Having never heard this line of argument, she was stuck in a state of trying to understand his point of view, leaving her speechless as she continued to listen.

Bic reinforced, "As a liberal, I'm telling you the whole argument of when a fetus has rights is arbitrary to the whims of society's values, sensitivities and self-interests, not logic, not truth, not science. Once the egg is fertilized, it will grow into a viable autonomous life. The whole idea that life doesn't start until the heart beats is insane. Are people who have artificial heart implants not alive? The whole idea that a fetus is not a life because it is dependent on the mother's womb is equally ridiculous. Infants are born and not attached, but are still completely dependent on others to survive. The whole idea that a fetus is not a life while at any developing state in the womb, also bunk. If you were two weeks pregnant, and some criminal punched you in the stomach so that the impact caused a miscarriage, you and most everybody would consider that murder. My position is that abortion is the intentional killing of a human being. It is no different in principle than killing a baby that is born or a child or an adult."

Finally, Bic summed up, "Society just doesn't care about the lives that the child bearer doesn't want. That may tear some people's feelings into a hypocritical frenzy, but I see no contradiction. Rights are not inherent, or 'self-evident,' they are granted by the consensus of the society."

***

"Oh, excuse me," said a man exiting the Starbucks as he nearly bumped into another gentleman wearing a trench coat and black fedora, looking somewhat from the Bogart era.

"Not an issue, fella," the anachronistic man replied.

Then the Starbuck's customer seemed to recognize the other man, "Hey." His eyes lit up. "I know you."

The other gentleman feigned a smile in return, thinking — not again.

"You're the guy who wrote this story!"

The author confessed, "Guilty."

"You're Cory Schulman, aren't you?"

"Yeah," he acknowledged curtly.

The customer gently put his hand up as if to halt the author. "I gotta say, I'm a little miffed at this story you thought up."

"Yeah?" the author questioned nearly dismissively.

"I mean, well, the story kind of...well I don't mean to be offensive, but it's just kind of boring. I mean you got a man who is obviously a thinly veiled version of you on a date that is way too intellectual to be believable. And it's you know upsetting, and taxing on the brain."

"So you don't like exploring issues, bud?"

"It's just that, what you got is a story that is just two people who would never be together talking their heads off for the entire book. Give me a break. That's boring."

"Look, man. I don't know your literacy level, but this book is for thinkers. Besides, eventually it picks up. Especially when the death occurs."

The customer was taken aback. "Death? Who dies?"

"You really don't expect me to spoil the story, do you?" The author looked at the customer anticipating an understanding.

"So, how's this story going to go?"

"Look, Sir," the author said bluntly. "You are the one walking out. If you want to learn who dies and who are the suspects, and what happens to these two main characters, then you just have to go back in, bite the bullet, and see what happens. And if you are too obtuse to patiently let a story unfold, then fuck it — walk out."

"Well, you don't have to get so touchy, Mr. Schulman. It's just so heady. The language so..."

"Pedantic, you yahoo. Now if you would excuse me, I'm trying to spy on my characters so I can see whether they're getting their lines right."

"Oh, oh, is it that Crazy Carl dude sleeping in the lounge chair? Is he the killer? Is it the robber?"

"Have a nice day fella." The author lifted his fingers in the air as if it's an effort to acknowledge the customer for the last time and resumed his clandestine snooping on Bic and Marisa.

***

After a great deal of patient listening to Bic's theories of rights and when life began, Marisa felt the urge to draw the conversation towards a more personal view. "Now here's a situation where I have some personal experience, not as a mother but as a therapist. Some of my patients have been in this predicament of an unwanted pregnancy and have suffered, agonized over the decision before a final action. And I've counseled them after some of them have made the decision to abort. Many of those women have life-long regret and as agonizing as it was to make the decision, the agony lasts for the remainder of their lives as a true weight on their conscience that can never be lifted."

Bic pounced again, "I never said people don't emotionally struggle with the decision and with whatever philosophical system they rely on, like religious doctrine. I'm just pointing out the fact that there aren't absolute rights and wrongs. There are the natural laws of physics and human consensus. We have what is possible and what we agree on. The rest of the debate of what's right and wrong is based on whatever paradigm of thought you latch onto and how that line of thinking creates restrictions for making your own conclusions. After all, if you believe that a God demands a certain way of living and to contradict that standard, you are wrong, then yes, you would be wrong to abort." Bic continued, "But I'm saying that the belief system is arbitrary. The premise dictates the conclusion. The premise of religion can be argued is arbitrary, but the laws of biology are a constant, and societal consensus is clear."

"Not from my point of view," Marisa defended. "I am a Jew. That comes with the Ten Commandments. That's clear to me. I don't have any conflict understanding and following the laws bestowed upon me. I'm simply asking where you stand. Don't you think a life is worth saving?"

"I'm not speaking to my own values," Bic said. "I'm just asking to what extent do we save unwanted lives?

Marisa reeled in his unending hypotheses and brought the discussion back to her point, "Don't you see through that? If killing an unborn life is acceptable, what would stop society from approving terminations of the born?"

"For one thing, we do," Bic affirmed. "It's called capital punishment, euthanasia, war-time assassinations, and collateral damage in the name of a military mission. But even without that, the answer is that our society finds killing the born unappealing."

Marisa took a moment to absorb this word "unappealing" and couldn't help but find it amusing. It's so common place, so whimsical. She wondered how Bic would explain that killing is restricted by being unappealing. She simply couldn't and hung her head in disengagement. She stretched her neck every which way and then looked up at Bic as she described him out loud. "You know Bic, you are the most profound idiot I've ever heard." Bic's eyebrows rose in surprise of her blatant insult.

She asked him, "Would you consider yourself morally bankrupt?"

Now it was Bic's turn to be incredulous, "Have you been here for the past hour? I don't believe in morality. It's a made-up concept by religion. People do good works because it is either in their self-interest or by some predisposition to empathize with others."

Marisa said "Okay. I think we are at an impasse with the whole right and wrong, blah blah blah issue. We're coming from two different ways of thinking and living. For me morality is clear and a self-evident truth of humanity. So, let's agree to talk less philosophically and more about things that directly affect our lives."

Bic shrugged indifferently. "Hey, like what? What do you think is relevant to our lives?"

Marisa started a new approach, "Being a woman naturally I find kids to be a central part of living. So, where do you stand on children?"

"If they are too loud, I stand on their tiny mouths. That usually shuts them up," Bic said proudly.

"Be serious."

Bic relaxed from his own commitment to talk about everything about life except the details of his own, then complained, "I'm seriously out of coffee. Would you like another cup?"

Appreciating the transition from the abstract discussion back to the realities of something tangible like coffee, Marisa accepted politely, "Sure, thanks Bic." But then she realized he never answered her question. "Actually, I was asking you about kids," she reminded him.

"Children: I am too old to bring more children into the world. I am 50 years old. If I brought a newborn into life, I may die by the time the kid is 20 when he or she could really benefit from guidance. That brings to mind, I did read a headline that the Chinese government is funding new research initiatives on head transplants. If that was available for me in 20 years, it could extend my life span to see a newborn of today well into his or her adult years."

"Head transplants?" Marisa burrowed her brow. "Yeah, that sounds like an option for you."

"Getting a little snarky, are we?" Bic bellyached. "Let me explain. A multi-disciplined team of researchers and surgeons have successfully transplanted a brown mouse's head onto a black mouse's body. And it survived. Think of the applications for humans who have immobile bodies due to spinal cord injuries and muscle-wasting diseases. They, as well as the general population, could get a renewed lease on life at the last stages of their lives. So long as their mind is lucid, they could get a whole new young body that could pump blood through their veins for decades to come."

Marisa tried to slow down Bic's rapid applications by questioning, "If all the bodies of recently deceased people are 'reapplied' for a lack of a better word, what would happen to organ donation? What about all the people who could benefit from the various organs of the donor's body?"

Bic saw no problem here. His confidence in medical advancements was unyielding. He qualified, "I'm sure by the time a head transplant is routine surgery, scientists will be able to grow individual organs per order."

Marisa sighed and said, "Have you ever thought about transplanting your head for a more intelligent one?"

Without losing a beat, Bic responded, "Yes I have, but to no avail. There just weren't any that were as profound and witty. So I'm stuck with the one I have." He then passed the question back to Marisa, "What are your thoughts on head transplants?"

Without giving the issue much serious thought, Marisa said dismissively, "It doesn't sit with me. I wouldn't want another body. I like the one I have."

Her answer didn't satisfy Bic who couldn't believe she didn't see the advantages of a transplant and pleaded, "But what if the one you have fails you? Suppose you have ALS or just so old that you are bedridden?”

“It’s just the idea,” she objected. “I wouldn’t want someone else’s body. It wouldn’t go with my head.”

Bic’s jaw dropped, “That’s your reason? Vanity? Really? So, vanity is your argument against head transplantation? You wouldn’t acknowledge the benefits of mobility and perhaps greater longevity. Think of it. You’re 90 years old and get a 20-year-old body. You could live another 50 years so long as your mind keeps working.”

She replied with resignation, “I think when I’m 90, I’ll be ready to die.”

“That’s just contrary to human instinct,” Bic complained. “Mostly anyway. I have nothing against self-termination if that’s desired and justifiable, as in assisted suicide when the future is hopeless, and the remainder of your life is both terminal and painfully agonizing — not to mention expensive. Frankly under those conditions, I would rather be able to leave my offspring some inheritance.”

Marisa shrugged.

Bic couldn't get off from the issue and finally said, "Forgive me, I just don't get your dependence on vanity as a justification for not living longer and with mobility. Heck, stick my head on a monkey body and I'll be happy." Marisa rolled her eyes. Bic continued, "And if someone touched me without my permission, I could say to them, 'Get your stink'n paws off me you damn, dirty ape.' Just as a joke."

Marisa squinted her eyes at Bic, "What are you babbling about?"

He looked back at her with incredulity, "Planet of the Apes. Hello? Charlton Heston? You don't get it? Ah, forget it." Bic gave up trying to convey the joke.

"You just want to live forever," Marisa accused. "I got news for you, mister. We're all mortal. We all die. What's beyond death, no one knows. That's where faith comes in. It gives rationality to an otherwise mysterious life."

Bic took issue again, "So you convince yourself there's more to life or after life than you could possibly know to comfort yourself while you're still alive. Don't you see? You are conning yourself, to make yourself feel secure when there's no logical reason to be secure. As you said, we're all going to die. And frankly, the pointlessness of one's life is subject to how they live it, not how they imagine it to be after it's over."

"You don't know that," she argued. Refusing to give an inch, Marisa replied, "People have been believing in God since the dawn of human kind. Now you think out of convenience you can dismiss it?"

"People have also been ignorant for thousands of years," Bic shot back. "Where and how do you think this faith crap gets concocted in the first place? It comes out of ignorance, to explain the inexplicable. Now with empiricism, we don't have to limit our perceptions of the unknown to our ancestors' fears and imaginations. We can study and determine the qualities and characteristics of the not yet known."

Again she felt the conversation had strayed from their lives. In an effort to bring him back to a more personal level, she said, "And what are your qualities and characteristics? Are you pontificating to avoid the truth about who you really are?"

Crazy Carl snorted and coughed. His body churned from side to side. His head wobbled as he awakened. His eyes blinked and to the shock of the baristas. He stood up, farted, peered at Marisa and Bic, then lumbered to the exit. Rebecca turned to Jimmy, "You are so lucky we didn't stick to the original bet."

He turned to her, "What do you mean? I would've won. The two geeks over there are still at it and the homeless guy is out of here."

"But that was what I bet. I'm the one who would've won."

"You don't know what you're talking about," Jimmy said. "Wait a minute. I forget already. Well, they've been here so freak'n long, no wonder we can't remember who said what. But anyway, that's not the bet is it? The bet is whether the guy gets another date with the girl. So get your hands ready for some weekend dishwashing," he taunted.

"Who am I, you ask?" Bic gently touched his chest with his fingertips. "Ah, a penetrating question from your analytical psychiatric side," Bic said. "I see the truth of life, capture it in novels, and connect with others by sharing my stories and insights with them. I employ words at my disposal and create a lyrical expression of the human condition."

That raised two questions in Marisa's mind. What exactly was so fascinating to Bic Penman and from where did he gather his thoughts? Was he a writer who relied on research, experience, observation, or other writers? She questioned him, "And you get your material from where?"

Bic leaned forward with focused attention and explained in a deliberate, hushed tone, "I delve into my personal experiences and recreate them, tailor them, twist them into a reality that suits me."

Marisa tried to sum up his reasons and performed a simple extrapolation, "So, in other words, reality is uncontrollable, unpredictable at times, even terribly low when it's not going your way, yet your writing enables you to control the conclusion in a way that comforts you? Sounds a lot like your argument against religion, don't you think?"

"Nice," Bic said. "You turned my criticism on religion unto myself. And now you expect me to weasel my way out of the apparent hypocrisy. Well, sorry to disappoint you. But I agree wholeheartedly. Writing is my bridge to meaning, control, and comfort. It is my religion. The difference is that my fiction is real, a real effort to create and a real expression of my insights and perceptions. Whereas your rituals and belief system are a hand-me-down story that never changes and so you, as a disciple, must conform to what others before you have told you is the Truth when they didn't have the foggiest idea of what Truth is."

Marisa took issue with Bic's dismissal of ritual, but instead of getting flustered, she seized the opportunity to educate her date. "You have no idea how significant ritual is, do you?"

Sensing he would be amused by what she had to say, Bic said, "Enlighten me."

She settled into a mentor's role, "Ritual enables you to acknowledge, honor, and appreciate everything in life, from the magnificent to the small detail." She paused and gathered her thoughts and with a positive glow, she continued, "When I say a blessing before drinking holy wine or eating a slice of bread, I am training my brain to take seriously what others would take for granted. When I pray, I am not only communicating to God and showing my obedience, I am also bringing my awareness of daily matters to a heightened level. I mean, the moment is not lost to a state of absent mindedness. Every moment, every action is acknowledged as significant."

"That's what I mean — do you hear yourself, Marisa? You seem to think there is only one way of interacting with the world. You say you want to be ever conscious of all matters, even the smallest detail like eating and drinking, so you don't take them for granted. I say that's fine for you and anyone who wants to dwell on minutia. But not me. I go out of my way to avoid small matters. I purposely buy all of the same kind of socks: all the same color and type — just so I don't have to waste time matching them and choosing from an array of different types. All I have to do is reach in my sock drawer and pull out two socks. Done! I'm on my way. I don't give it a second's thought, by design. That's what I want. I don't want to waste time, attention, and energy for something that hardly matters. That doesn't mean I don't appreciate wearing socks. I do like wearing socks. I'm just more interested in thinking about other matters. And as you can witness, my lack of conscientious ritual did not render me barefooted today."

"Sounds like you put a lot of thought into your sock theory."

Bic reflected a moment and continued his justifications. "Instead of unnecessarily magnifying the importance of the minutia, the 'true believers' should make sure they actually follow what they preach. The true hypocrites are the ones ensconced in religion who do unrighteous things, like embezzle from the church funds or cheat on their spouses. Then they run to confession or whatever religious loophole they can get to be forgiven. That may alleviate the guilt, but it doesn't make them less of a hypocrite."

Marisa showed signs of fatigue from Bic's immersion into issues that don't get to the heart of who he is on a concrete, personal level. So, she tried again, "So Shakespeare, what have you written that's so mellifluous to the ear and enduring for the ages?"

"All right," he said. "Fair enough. You want to hear something I've written that can withstand the test of time. How's this? When I was a college student 30 years ago, I wrote a short poem. This is it:"

Vivid imagery encourages passivity;
inattentive mind prevents activity.
Eyes are open, locked in place;
mind is closed, released in space.

Marisa scrunched up her face, "That's it? You were, what, describing someone watching television?"

Feeling self-conscious, Bic said, "Yes sort of. More like daydreaming. Awake but absent at the same time." He awaited hopefully for an evolution of Marisa's reaction.

After a moment of polite reflection Marisa said, "Uh. I'm not sure that really qualifies as a timeless gem."

Defensively Bic replied, "Hey, I never said poetry was my strong point. Besides, I was in college. It's supposed to suck. Try this one:"

A Poet's Principle Value

I do know all and all, the mind will decide
whether to trip or dance, defy or abide.
Thought and art peak intensity
out from latent burial during stability.

Marisa took in a deep breath then slowly puffed out her cheeks as she blew out the air. "Okay, I've interpreted dreams in my practice as a licensed psychotherapist, so I'm going to say you are trying to say creativity is linked to a state of instability."

"Yes. Well, isn't it?" Bic replied seriously. "I mean, don't you have stronger realizations and insights when things go haywire? I mean, all of my ideas come from the extremes of life. I need to differentiate the daily grind into meaningful feelings. I need to witness people's foibles, hypocrisy, and self-imploding efforts. I need to be screamed at, admonished, and unfairly treated to connect with the realities of imperfection. Then I have something to say, and I have something to write about."

Seizing on a glaring contradiction in Bic's whole perception and reasoning, she questioned, "So how do you derive any thoughts from a boring job?"

Bic tried to explain his ideas, "When my life is idle, I start to go a little stir crazy and my mind tries to compensate by exploding with elaborate thoughts. Twenty-first century living is too ridiculous for how humanity has evolved. We sit on chairs staring at computer screens for eight and half hours a day and then sit in traffic another hour to get home, then sit in front of the television because we're too exhausted from our sedentary and cognitively debilitating lives."

Marisa attempted again, "Sounds to me that you create an elaborate philosophy to dress up your state of inactivity. Ultimately, it looks like you have become a fatalistic depressive."

Unfazed, Bic didn't fight back but instead simply said, "Maybe. Seeing reality for the routine that it is, is depressing. It is up to us to create our own drama. So we travel and lean on entertainers. We go to bars and get wasted so that the ugly girl at 7:00 pm looks like a solitary angel at closing. Anything to change our perceptions from honest objectivism to that of self-delusion. That's the only way most people can handle the mediocrity of life. But to artists, scientists, people who can change the status quo, life is more interesting, because we see things, we create them, and when we leave the earth, our legacy remains for the ages."

Marisa took another crack at a summation, "Sounds to me that your creativity is rooted in complaints on modern life. You're so pissed off that life has an end that you spend all your time griping about it. And you think your gripes translate into literature that will in some way make you immortal. Well then, what else have you done?"

Bic's eyes looked upward as he tried to think of another example of his writing. Then an expression of discovery enlivened his face. "Okay. I title this one: 'Life After Death.'" Bic looked into Marisa's eyes and began to recite his poem:

> Today, a day to be
> 22 years for Annabelle
> though not for the last three.
>
> From the past is Annabelle
> today memory lives to tell
> though her birthday should be
> for three years she's gone free.
>
> Annabelle's younger sister,
> Patricia, turns 20
> and sees
> a picture now
> of Annabelle then.
>
> All the wonder to be older
> than your sister elder.

"What's with your obsession of life after death?" she blurted out with a tinge of frustration.

"I have observations….," he explained, "that lead me to whatever conclusion or issue that I see. In this case, I was friends with this beautiful dancer who just had a birthday at 20, which made her older than her older sister because her older sister died at the age of 19. So, I thought it was a bit weird to be older than your older sister. The younger sister got the chance to live beyond the point that her older sister died, hence life after death."

Marisa sighed.

"Hey look Marisa, I just recited a few short poems that I did as a college freshman. That's not to say they represent my writing style and themes of today. I've had 30 years of living, thinking, and developing since then. Would you rather I recite one of my 300-page novels? We're on a meet and greet, not a semester-long educational retreat."

"And frankly," Bic continued unto yet another diatribe, "living longer than an older sibling is the only life after death I believe in. It's not so much that I'm obsessed with death as I am obsessed with life and what to do with it while I have it, while I'm healthy. So much of life is wasted. I am driven to experience the drama and cite the inconsistencies that make individual philosophies incomplete and typically ridiculous.

***

The author cloaked in a black trench coat and hat cupped his hands around his eyes as he peered through the Starbuck's window observing his characters when from behind him, he hears someone shout: "Mr. Schulman! Mr. Schulman!" The former customer who had walked out of the story came back hurriedly. The writer turned around to hear the other man ask, "What's going on now? What's happening? Did someone get killed yet?"

"Aren't you bored with my abstruse issues, esoteric dialogue, and Falstaffian wit?" the author replied somewhat rhetorically, then answered the customer's question, "No. No one's bit the dust just yet."

"Did you save it for the climax?"

"Na. But it's going to happen soon enough. Just hang in there."

"Mind if I watch with you, Mr. Schulman?"

"Sure, just be discreet."

Just then, a passerbyer noticed the two men staring into the Starbucks which raised her curiosity. "Whuch y'all lookin at?" she asked innocently enough.

The customer turned around and explained the situation. Then there were three huddled together looking through the Starbuck's window.

***

Marisa refocused on Bic and interjected, "And what makes you so righteous that you're above hypocrisy and sin?"

"The difference is that if I do something unethical, I don't deny it or rationalize it," Bic said. "I don't dress it up with elaborate excuses. It's like the arguments against gay marriage. Religious-minded folks pose a phony argument against gay marriage that 'God didn't create Adam and Adam.' And that marriage is defined as a contract between a man and a woman. This is utterly ridiculous when marriage is a made-up concept to begin with. And it can be defined any way a society wants it to be."

Marisa tried to counter his argument in a general way, "Religion helps people cope with life. It helps people make sense out of the world. For example, if a loved one gets murdered for no reason, religion helps people survive and move on."

Bic's confidence returned easily enough. He laughed mockingly, "I never said self-deception wasn't soothing. It's just so primal in respect to what we now know about the world and life."

"Are you saying you wouldn't reach out to God and pray if you were in a plane that was about to crash?" she asked.

"If I ever did that, it would be nothing more than a statement of trepidation and fragility and have absolutely nothing to do with a rational perspective about cause and effect," he said without hesitation.

Marisa tried a different approach to reach an emotional connection with Bic, "All right, suppose you were in a plane crash and everybody died except you. Then would you believe?"

"No, of course not. Why would I?" he said bluntly. "Hundreds of other people, innocent people would have perished. Why would I believe in a God that would allow hundreds of innocent people to die just to spare my life? I would chalk it up to dumb luck." Then Bic returned to a cockiness that was always just below his surface, "I'll tell you what — if I survive 10 consecutive plane crashes, I will convert."

Marisa challenged Bic, "So how do you live life? How do you navigate through a world of chance? Where do you exercise your free will?"

"First of all, I try not to board rickety planes," Bic said slyly. "Secondly, I reconcile my own initiative to what the world has to offer." Before Marisa had a chance to ask what the hell he meant, he preempted her. "For example, I determined the qualities of the woman I wanted on the dating website. Your name came up among others. So in essence, I determined the outcome by selecting you to contact. But whether we are a successful couple depends not just on what I want; it's an integration with your free will — coupling of two independent wills. That creates an unending force of unpredictability. For at any time one of us could divert from the common ground we have established."

"Hold that thought for a moment. I have to divert to the little girl's room," she said. Marisa got up and left. A patron sitting nearby leaned over to Bic and interjected, "You seem to be getting along with your date."

Bic shot back fatalistically, "That's because we each know we can get out of our seat at any time and bolt out of here without ever seeing each other again."

Marisa returned from the bathroom, "A thought occurred to me that you say you want to capture life's special moments and share them with others for eternity. So how is it you experience life when all you're doing in essence is recording it? It's like you are content filming a live football game and later showing the highlights. Is that truly living a life by just taking notice of highlights? Don't you ever want to actually play the game? It's like you sit around thinking about how you can be insightful to justify your own existence, when the fact that you are here and alive is testimony to your existence. So that leads me to believe you're more concerned with life after death than you are about the here and now."

Bic shrugged, "You don't think I participate in life? I don't live a daily grind? I do all the things necessary to responsibly take care of myself. And it is utterly a near complete waste of grey matter, time, effort, and a violation of any rational standard of living."

Marisa summed up his argument, "In other words you work at a job that you hate."

Bic defended his situation, "Well, I can't afford to retire at 50. I work because I have to, not because I think I am an integral part of society. Believe me, I'm dispensable at work as is everyone else. No matter how hard I work, I will be nothing more than a replaceable employee at a $4 billion corporation."

"See what I mean?" she said with building confidence. "You are overcompensating for an underwhelming life. Since you're so undervalued, you have to devise a complicated counter philosophy to balance things out. You create your own perfected reality through your written works because your real life sucks."

"Is that the Physician's Desk Reference diagnosis, 'my real life sucks?'" Bic questioned. "Hey I can't realistically make a living just being a poet, playwright, or novelist. I have to parlay my writing skill into something practical that pays me a salary I can live on. It's not my fault. That's capitalism. And so what if I draw creative expression from my depressing circumstances? I don't see any hypocrisy in that. If I were happy at my work, who knows, I might draw inspiration from that situation too."

Remembering his poem that suggested creativity is derived from turmoil, she quoted, "I thought your creativity only comes out 'from latent burial during stability?' Don't you have to be a little crazed to be creative?"

"Believe me, I'm constantly crazed. I'm only stable-minded enough to collect a paycheck. And, the only way I can tolerate being underemployed is to use it as fodder for my artistic expression," Bic said in earnest.

"So you turn your vulnerabilities into strengths," she said in a way that was more palatable to Bic's acceptance.

"Look, I'll be the first to say I'd much rather have a job that I was passionate about. But in the writing field, the interesting, high paying jobs are rare."

"I don't know," Marisa shook her head disapprovingly. "If I wasn't passionate about what I do on a daily basis I would go insane."

Bic returned to his personal philosophy, "From where I stand, the more insane one is the more they are in touch with a creative outlet."

"You wouldn't say that if you had to be institutionalized," she retorted from personal experience as a therapist for patients who were institutionalized.

Bic showed one of his palms in honesty, "I have been institutionalized."

Taken back, Marisa blurted out, "For what?"

"I was listless and uncommunicative for about a week after smoking dope that probably was laced with something much stronger," he explained.

"You were a stoner?" she asked.

Bic explained, "On rare occasions I smoked marijuana back in my high school and college days. One night in a college dorm room, I got high. Time slowed and I focused on the granular taste of eating a chocolate bar. Time shifted per second. My perception seemed like I was looking at old film footage that flickered with each passing frame. It was surreal. Then I fell asleep. The next morning, I got up and walked across campus without any issue. It was early and nobody was around. I didn't interact with anyone until reaching my therapist's office where I had a standing weekly session. We sat down and then I just fell over to the side. She called for the ambulance and before I knew it, I was in a psych ward. I couldn't talk and showed signs of fear and paranoia. I would shrink away when nurses approached."

"So were you a creative genius then?" she asked half mockingly, half inquisitive.

"I did produce some interesting art on paper," Bic said. "At the time during my college days, I used to draw on an art pad. And when I was in the psych ward, I attempted to draw myself. My perceptions and coordination were so discombobulated that my renderings looked like a disabled person or little kid drew them. My pictures looked like depictions of grotesque deformities. But with each passing day at the hospital, my drawings became more and more anatomically accurate as my mind returned to normal. The evolution from dysfunction to clarity in my artistic montage made an interesting artistic statement."

A little lost, Marisa asked, "Yes? The statement being what?"

He continued, "The lifecycle of losing a grip on reality. I could never have captured that sequence of devolving and returning to normalcy without that experience. As for now, I experience turmoil from living a completely ordinary and underwhelming lifestyle. That's okay though. Instead of writing about the terror of hand-to-hand combat in the war zone, I will have to be content about writing about a bowl of fruit."

Marisa exhaled, "Okay, I think I was keeping up with you until we got into hand-to-hand combat and fruit."

Bic sipped hot coffee from his straw, taking a moment to recollect his thoughts on the matter and tried again to explain. "As a writer, there's nothing out of the ordinary or unique about my life. In other words I have not experienced anything as dramatic as hand-to-hand combat. But it's my ability to selectively identify a story worth telling and telling it in a unique way that gives rise to my talents. In other words, my life may be no more dramatic than a simple bowl of fruit. But as we all know, talented artists can paint mundane objects such as a bowl of fruit and create a masterpiece."

"You have no shortage of self-admiration, I see," said Marisa.

"What can I say? I'm my biggest fan," Bic admitted shamelessly. "The fact that I think of my writing as good, doesn't conflict with my commitment to objectivity. I am that good."

"If objectivity is your best quality, what's your worst?" Marisa asked.

"Quality?" Bic asked, then clarified, "I see reality too clearly. It's depressing. Do you know what life is like when you can't rationalize away your problems? To know that a terrible situation is truly terrible? Because I'm so analytical and self-aware, if I ever try to rationalize away a problem, I would fail miserably, because I would be aware that I was rationalizing. This awareness pre-empts self-delusion."

Sensing Bic was exaggerating his suffering, she challenged, "Oh, is living in the United States, the most advanced, richest, and most powerful nation on earth so terrible? Aren't you a fortunate person for just being born here?"

"Yes I am, but that's no panacea for happiness and fulfillment. All the wealth, luxury and security are no match for knowing deep down that everything is temporary and that as the years pass, we all slowly degenerate. The greatest life on earth is destined to die no differently than the poorest wretch on earth."

"Are we back to that again?" Marisa asked. "What happened to 'Life's a journey' and what inspires the intellect of Bic Penman, besides freshman poetry?"

"Fair enough," Bic said. "I wrote a collection of vignettes, each finding the essence of a childhood memory."

"This was, what, an autobiography?" she asked.

"Sort of," Bic said. "The memories really occurred, but I wrote them as fiction to make them more entertaining to readers."

Marisa made an inquiry suspecting there was more to Bic Penman than a bowl of fruit, "Did you have an unusual childhood?"

"No, actually it was pretty typical," he admitted. "Nothing any more or less interesting than anyone else's childhood. The book's success lies in the story telling of ordinary experiences so that it intrigues the reader. At the same time, a story is told that amuses or exposes the innocence of a boy who is first learning about life.”

“Like what for example?” she wanted to learn something in particular rather than philosophical babble or other intellectual pontificating.

At first Bic was inhibited to share. “Oh, taken out of context it wouldn’t be as entertaining,” Bic first said. But compelled to share his work, he elaborated, “But just as a small example, one of the vignettes describes the time I was about 10 years old and woke up after having a disturbing dream. At the breakfast table, I told my family I had dreamt that a snake had slithered across my neck. They laughed and so after eating a plate of syrup-drenched pancakes, I went outside to pick up some flagstones and collect worms in a paper cup. Then I brought them upstairs to feed my pet Garter snake, but when I got to the cage, my snake was gone! I leave it up to the reader’s imagination as to what really happened. The story illustrated the comingling of the imagined with the real.”

Rebecca asked Jimmy, "What's going on now? What's the odds looking like?"

Jimmy estimated, "I'd say still touch and go here. He got all poetic at one point and then they talked about God and drugs, but she's still there. So maybe they are into each other. I don't get it though. She's arguing with him tooth and nail. He's just talking his head off. This is truly the date that never ends."

Jimmy looked at Rebecca, "I think I'll surrender."

"You're giving up? That means I win."

"Not exactly. Let's make a deal. I'll take over your Saturday shift, if we call off the bet."

"Why are you giving up?"

"Look at them. Listen to them. They just don't shut up. They just keep going. They'll be here after closing. Let's just say, any woman who can tolerate a man that much into himself, must be into him."

"Deal."

Marisa looked at Bic and decided to penetrate and uncover his passion. "So, Mr. Penman, what is it about literature that gets you so enamored?"

Bic, feeling the conversation was back on home court advantage, welcomed the question. "Literature, in essence, is a long example of a thought," Bic started off. "I have lots of thoughts that need context for them to make sense. So, literature is the perfect format. It enables me to write about any subject whether it be a criticism about culture, circumstances, decisions, history. It's a platform by which I can assert an opinion, state a fact, question a circumstance, or just capture a piece of reality. I can describe, characterize, or voice an attitude. I can scheme and plot and determine the outcome of any situation. And I can do all this while romancing the written word into lovely, creative passages that titillate the mind."

Marisa wasn't satisfied with his general answer. She pressed him for something more revealing. "But what exactly are you passionate about? Surely, you have to choose a subject at some point," she said.

"I've gotten to the point of my life where I just want to live purposefully and with insight into meaningful experiences. This is opposed to a goal-driven life. Not to say goals aren't important, but they just shouldn't be the end all. The process toward the goal should be equally satisfying. The 'along-the-way' should be quite a tour of life."

"Is that a circuitous way of saying 'Life's a journey'"?

"Say it any way you want, Marisa. It may be clichéd, but the process is just as significant as the goal. In that vein, I intend to travel and see the world, talk to people who are different than me and who think differently."

Marisa sighed, "So you're discontented with the United States of America too?"

"Well, it's like whatever society you live in, it indoctrinates you."

"Even in the land of the free, Bic?"

"Yes," he said. "Even in the USA. We're indoctrinated by the media and culture driven by big business and advertisers. Ever notice that the various news stations all cover the same issues, and only the ones that are most sensational like disasters, killings, abuses, political turmoil, wars, financial and economic troubles. It gets monotonous. And depending on which network you tune into will determine the bias you receive. Fox News, for example, will certainly slant the news to suggest the Democrats are running the nation into the ground. Republican-minded people watch that biased commentary and it reinforces what they think they know."

"So, what," she said. "Everybody thinks their way of thinking is the right way. That's why they have come to the positions they hold close to heart. But, to take a page out of your book, doesn't science give a common ground for everybody to agree on things? I mean in the physical world, not speaking spiritually now, just particles and physics."

"Well, not so fast," Bic cautioned. "It's like each political party interprets the science to fit their positions. The Republicans say fracking is safe because they support big oil companies. The Democrats say it's polluting our water tables and causing earthquakes. Besides, science is inconclusive because what seems evident today is incorrect later with additional understandings from more sophisticated studies."

"So even the great Bic Penman who drapes himself in the physical world, doubts the discipline of science and recognizes its limitations," she said.

"Hey, science is only valid if it is conducted with integrity by those who use it. Secondly, science is a continuum of learning. I never said a particular scientific discovery is the end all of everything," he claimed.

"I was under the impression that you think everything can be solved through technological solutions," she said.

"Theoretically, perhaps," Bic said. "But look, there's a human factor along the way. People don't agree on the solutions to problems. A solution to one problem can create another problem. It's like this," he said. "We used to get paper bags from the grocery store. Then the environmentalists start screaming in the name of protecting trees. They put a stop to the paper bags so loggers don't strip away our forests. Enter the plastic bag. Now trees are saved by the replacement of non-biodegradable plastic that will remain in landfills for about a thousand years. Hence another problem."

"Okay," Marisa agreed cautiously not knowing where Bic was heading with this.

Bic felt he hadn't made a strong enough case for his thought, so he conjured up another example. "Computers enabled us to go paperless. Great! Less trees are cut down, but now battery acid from all of the discarded computers leaks into the freshwater tables in the landfills. There is always a belief that the next technological advancement will repair a problem, but only causes more damage."

"You don't believe in science either? My patients, and you too, depend on the scientific advancements to treat psychiatric disorders," she countered.

He rebutted her position, "Pharmaceutical waste, pesticides, and antibiotics designed to help us, contaminate the food supply chain and the drinking water. The contamination to our waterways causes fish to devolve into asexual forms that are unable to reproduce which affects the entire ecosystem."

Bic couldn't contain himself. He began a ranting diatribe that saw no end. He jumped to the next bothersome conflicting thought, "Nuclear energy designed to provide cheap power is the most ridiculous. First, we have to spend millions upon millions of dollars to build a power plant. The radioactive waste will remain deadly for about 10,000 years. So, to get rid of it, the government plans to transport it from all parts of the country by trucks to Nevada and bury it under Yucca Mountain, which is only 90 miles south of the populated city of Las Vegas. Besides the vulnerability of power plants to attack, now we will have hundreds of trucks crisscrossing the country that will also be vulnerable to attack or accident. On top of that the damn things have to be built and operated safely. Despite reassurances of safety measures and redundant safety mechanisms, Three-Mile Island happened, Chernobyl happened, and Fukushima happened. Not to dismiss the ultimate stupidity of building these things on earthquake faults, near densely populated cities, or near the ocean. What can you expect but eventual disaster?"

Marisa glared at Bic, "Are you finished standing on your soapbox? So, what's your solution? Windmills in every back yard?"

"Solar energy, ocean currents, waterfalls, wind farms, they all could be used," he said.

"Ever get the feeling that you talk about the world's problems just to avoid your true feelings of worthlessness?"

"Yes, of course," Bic admitted. "What else can people do but distract themselves from the inevitable realization that life is relatively pointless? That as individuals we have limited options for change and influence. To march in protest among thousands of others, does what exactly? Promote public awareness, show solidarity? Sure, but frankly too many things are just screwed up." Bic sighed, then continued, "Society has solutions to most of its problems. It's just implementation against the status quo. Big business has a foothold on their current revenue streams. Like the energy sector is entrenched in the use of fossil fuels. To introduce cheaper, better solutions is to disrupt the existing form of profit. And they have lobbyists that ensure that the lawmakers make it difficult to uproot the established forces."

Marisa was certain Bic was avoiding attention to his personal qualities by deflecting attention to external issues of the world. She put him to the task, "So what are you doing to save the world, my distracted friend? Or do you put all of your faith in humankind's efforts to solve their problems with the next technological advancement?"

"Yes, sort of. That's the way it's been so far," he said. "Take for example, the pesticide run off into the freshwater streams. That may be a moot point if we convert traditional flat farms to vertical farms. Think of food-bearing plants growing in stacked troughs as high as a skyscraper in controlled conditions. They would be fed the appropriate minerals and water in just the right proportions not depending on the next arbitrary rain. The green house would protect them from insect invasions and disease, not to mention unseasonable freezes and strong storms."

Now Bic's thoughts raced with other examples. "Look, not only will self-driving cars help avoid accidents and unnecessary fatalities, but I assure you the next technological revolution will result in ubiquitous androids performing the tasks no one else really wants to do."

Giving into Bic's futuristic frontier, Marisa suggested the inevitable downside. "And what's going to happen when these androids replace the clerks and such? Won't that impact the employment sector? Would capitalism even work at that point?" she hypothesized.

Without missing a beat, Bic said "Of course it will. Things will resettle into a new normal that's all."

"What do you mean?" she asked.

"I mean, we will adjust. For example, we don't have to have a 40-hour work week in America. The Europeans have about 6 weeks off every year. Americans get two weeks off. If we lessoned the number of hours required to work every week or increased time off for vacation, more people would have to be hired. Likewise, if we reintroduced the draft for non-combat roles, we could remove an entire generation from the work force. We would need androids at that point to fill the void in the labor market."

Marisa didn't give up. She knew she could get Bic to reveal his essence so she asked him, "So you have all the answers, right? All the criticisms, but what are you actually doing about anything?"

"I do what I do," he said. "I'm not an engineer or politician, inventor, or anybody else who can contribute to solving these matters. My only talent is writing, so that's what I do. My perceptions, my storytelling, my acrobatic thinking and word juggling make me the one-man talent show when it comes to making a book."

"Talent show? Don't you mean "circus?"

"Listen, a book that brings minds together. A book that rallies the masses and brings emotion and passion to an issue, so apathy gives way to awareness and awareness to action. That's what I can do; that's what I am doing; that's all I can do. And that's good enough for me. Life may be futile in the end, but while we are alive, things matter. We're all connected in a

118

global sphere that is only divided by made-up culture, made-up borders, and made-up laws. At some point we will realize that no one owns anything, that we are all borrowers, until the next person assumes that role. And if we want our lives to matter, even in a temporary way, we must make that meaning for ourselves. Meaning is illusive because it is self-proclaimed. It is the characterization of what we decide to do in the face of ultimate futility."

"So how do you stay happy Bic, with the ultimate demise lurking in everyone's inevitable future?"

"Happiness?" he questioned. "That's an ephemeral emotion that I reserve for special moments, rather than as a state of mind."

"So, you intentionally deprive yourself of happiness?" she asked. "Why are you bothering to live then?"

"Not for the peripheral satisfaction of happiness," he said. "Depressives don't stay happy for long. We pride ourselves on seeing the world through realistic perspectives. Objectivity is cruel. You see the world and situations for what it is. You can't give me a trophy for showing up to a competition. I would actually have to do something remarkable like win the competition to feel that I accomplished something. You see. You can't con me into being happy. It has to happen organically."

"Well, if you weren't so rigid in your beliefs, if you had a little faith in the unknown, maybe you could be happy," she offered.

"Hey! Maybe if I dropped acid every day, I could be deliriously happy all day. But self-delusional faith would be just as nonsensical as the happiness one feels through artificial, drug-induced delirium. I have to do something really spectacular, something that awes me, to feel happy. I have to fight through the writing process and capture an insight and express it beautifully, originally — to feel the spiritual elation you seem to get by clasping your hands together and speaking to an imagined super being that has nothing better to do than listen to your feeble thoughts and anxieties."

Marisa smiled and deferred the insult. "So, have you done that, Bic? Have you written anything that gives you that elated feeling?"

"That's my quest. That's my lifelong journey, my process. It's my nemesis, my great white whale; my reason for getting out of bed. It's my obsession: to find a message worthy of conveyance to anyone who will listen and write it in a manner that compels them to listen. This effort requires not only the passion to write, but the passion to live as well. In other words, writers must experience as much life as possible outside their comfort zone to understand the complexities, the connections, the range of emotions and thoughts from as many different perspectives as possible. They must assume the body and minds of others who live different lives and speak in their own patterned ways. Writers describe life in all of its contradictions and surprising arbitrariness. But you want specifics, right?" he asked.

She nodded expectantly.

"You want to know if I've written anything that would interest you. Well, I have written two plays, about 20 poems, perhaps 60 biographies, four novels, numerous newspaper articles, and two reference books. None of them have made much noise in the marketplace, so it's unlikely you would have come across any of them. But, you know, I do this not for fame or fortune, but rather because that's what I do. I am a writer. Words excite me. Why is this? I don't know why I have this disposition, but I do and I wouldn't be whole doing something else."

"Don't you see? That's how I feel about my faith and my psychotherapy," Marisa said.

"I have no doubt," Bic said. "I'm not judging you, Marisa, just because I find faith ridiculous. If it makes sense to you, why not? If you think clasping your hands in prayer has some sort of causal factor on anything, go ahead. Maybe you can pick stocks that way and pray for a high return on investment."

"You are judging me through your derision," she pointed out.

"Yes, you're right; I am judging you. But that's part of the benefit of pursuing the truth. And that's what I seek. The stark truth. Not for happiness but for the world to make sense. I'd rather face an ugly truth than believe in a delightful lie," he explained.

Bic continued in a morbid depiction. "The reality is that life is a slow degeneration of mind and body until self-awareness is terminated. Our mind stops and our bodies decay. And every effort given forth up until then is no longer counted," he said.

Marisa took issue with Bic. "But that's your choice to believe in the nothingness of your life. And, you wallow in its hollowness, its emptiness. Who wouldn't? It's a terrible thought to assume that life is without meaning, without an enduring impact after our physical lives finish. Why do you think religion has flourished for 5,000 years?"

"Give me a break, will you Marisa? We had this conversation already. Stupidity has also flourished for 5,000 years."

"And it's continuing right now as I listen to you," she replied. "Enough, enough about reality," she said excitedly. "So, what are you doing in reality? How are you living? Tell me something specific, real, and down to earth.”

***

Outside the Starbucks, a number of persons noticed the author and his fans intently observing the inside happenings of the coffee shop. With their curiosities teased, others joined in the spectatorship. As the group of onlookers acquired new members, it took on a life of its own attracting more and more attention as still others stopped to explore the fascination of Marisa and Bic.

Amongst the small mob of persons, one shouted, “Which one is going to get killed? Let it be Bic.”

Another shouted back, “No, he’s the one who represents reason and logic. If he died, that would mean life has no coherence.”

“What are you saying? If Marisa dies, wouldn’t it mean there is no justification for God and faith?”

Still another voice said, “You’re both wrong. This is a comedy.”

“No, it’s a tragedy.”

“No, It’s a romance of two opposite people.”

As the crowd argued the nature of the story, the writer shushed the crowd and yelled, "Quiet. We don't want to distract the characters."

***

"Sounds like you're asking me what my hobbies are," he said.

"Well?" Marisa looked at him with encouragement.

"Well okay, on the weekends, I like to wake up early and lounge at Starbucks with a 12-ounce cup of their morning blend. I take one sugar, whole milk, and leisurely nurse it through a thin straw for about an hour while I read magazines, books, or the paper."

"Sitting around a coffee shop is a hobby?" she asked.

"I like to read," he said. "That's what I'm getting at. I take interest in new technological and medicinal developments, political movements, golf, tennis, and football news, etc. I also attend plays every once in a while at the Arena and Round House theatres. I actually see the plays free of charge because I volunteer as an usher. Yeah, I show people to their seats and answer inane questions, like 'where is seat C-105?' 'It's next to seat C-106! Here, take a playbill.'"

A pause in the conversation caused Bic to conjure another example. "Of course, an interesting museum is always close at heart."

She still wanted specifics that were not based on the intellect. "So what do you actually do other than entertain yourself with other people's takes on life?"

Bic dug deep into his history to start off with activities that have long ago disappeared from his daily regimen. "Okay, well, that's been different over the years. Well, you know I was a former thespian."

"You? Really? Like what, TV commercials?" she said with heavy doubt.

"No. Live performances on stage. In the second grade, I was a tree."

"Oh, I see Mr. Jokester. Still trying to get me to snort coffee up my nose, are you?"

"You see, my acting is rooted in the tree." He looked at her in earnest. "I expected to branch out from there."

"Ha Ha. Seriously. Tell me something personal."

"Okay, after college, I went into real estate and became a multi-million-dollar agent within two years. Then started my business as a writer which lasted fifteen years. In the meantime, I bought a house, married and had a daughter and wrote my first book. Next, I divorced, was diagnosed with Tourette's, and have been in a medicated daze ever since, which is one reason I gave up my business and now work for a large conglomerate insane asylum that pays me a ridiculously high salary to do a ridiculously small amount of meaningless work."

Marisa reflected in admiration and summarized, "A successful businessman? And, a homeowner to boot? Sounds like you've done okay for yourself Bic." She probed, "So what ideas do you ponder other than death and dying? Something where you made a critical difference in something or someone's life."

"What do you want me to say, that I saved a choking man in a restaurant by administering the Heimlich maneuver? That I leave gifts for kids living in a homeless shelter? That I discovered the cure for cancer? I'm sorry but we all can't be the quintessential citizen who deserves a lifelike statue on public grounds. No one is going to name a school after me and guess what? That's okay, because I create my own reality through my books," he explained.

"Do you substitute the mundanity of real living with storytelling so you can live vicariously through fictional success?" she asked.

"Hey, sue me for being ordinary," Bic replied. "Why do you think storytelling has been so prevalent throughout the ages? It shows us the full dimension of life even if we only experience a perfunctory sliver of it. Our intellectual curiosity and our emotional hunger crave insight into others so that we know there is more to life than just sitting around a coffee shop and sloggin' into a job you don't care about every day."

"So where do you want to take this?" Marisa got to the point.

"Huh?" Bic looked at Marisa wide-eyed as if looking at her for the first time.

"Do you want a second date, 'Mr. Live for Today' and for the rest of eternity?"

Rebecca swept the floor with a straw broom and overheard Marissa's proposal. She scurried over to Jimmy and whispered the situation in his ear.

"The bet is off, remember?" Jimmy said.

"Just saying," Rebecca replied.

"Uh. Well," Bic hesitated, "you didn't really tell me how you spend your time."

"I spend my time gardening, cleaning, work, synagogue, you know the 'perfunctory lifestyle' you were railing against," she said.

Bic floundered in indecision. "So, I don't know. What do you envision for us?"

"I envision eating a very green salad at a very nice restaurant and listening to you babble about how your elaborate philosophy masks your fear of intimacy. You say you were married. What happened?" Marisa seized another opportunity to get to the essence of Bic Penman.

"Now you're getting personal," he said defensively.

"It is a date."

Bic replied with greater precision on the characterization of their meeting at Starbucks. "This is a meeting to determine whether we can stand the sight of each other without running in the opposite direction; we're still negotiating the date."

She used his logic to justify her position, "Well neither one of us has run out — that's a sign, don't you think? You're not negotiating a deal with the devil, remember. You don't believe in all that superstition."

Almost with reluctance, Bic overcame his inhibition. "What do you like to eat?"

"I'm a vegetarian," she said.

"Wonderful, salads won't tax my wallet much," he said without shame, oblivious that he, in essence, was broadcasting that he was 'tight with money.'

Then Marisa inquired, "What do you like to eat?"

"Anything that swims, runs, or flies," he said.

"Do you like Indian food?" she asked.

"I like any and all food," Bic said. He reflected a moment and asked, "Where's this leading? A walk down the aisle? Screaming kids jumping on me first thing in the morning? A crushing mortgage to pay every month?"

"It's just a date," she reassured. "If a serious relationship scares you so much, why are you on a dating site?" she asked.

Bic shot back, "I'm just curious as to what people actually look like in contrast to their ten-year-old pictures they post on the site."

"Ha, ha," she laughed. "Well, you signed up now you're committed. That's the obligation."

"You mean just because I agreed to meet you, I am obligated to take you out?"

"The fact that you didn't jump out of your seat and escape mid-way through means you're interested. Surprise, you qualify to take me out," she toyed with him.

Bic mused for a moment aloud, "Hmmm. I guess I can't take my money with me when I die."

"No, you can't."

"So, I suppose I can take you out. But I can tell you right now, I'm not getting married, Marisa."

"Okay, I promise you don't have to marry me on our second date."

"Ever! I don't believe in that. If two people love each other they can just be together until they don't want to anymore. It's a lot cheaper. No $300 an hour divorce attorney."

"You're quite the romantic, aren't you?"

"I know how to press my lips against yours."

"Bic, are you seriously deconstructing kissing?"

"I mean, I know how to kiss. Just you wait until we lock lips. You'll be seeing some romance that you won't forget. I'll ruin you for anyone else."

"Looking forward to it."

"Mmmm. Okay. I'll see you again. What do you want to do?"

"You'll think of something," she said instilling more confidence in Bic than Bic perhaps had in himself.

"Fine. Dinner and a movie?"

Jimmy gently smacked Rebecca on the shoulder in disbelief.

Somewhat unimpressed, Marisa challenged, "You can be more creative than that can't you? You're a creative artist."

"Fine. Dinner, a movie, and popcorn. Don't ask me for butter too, or I'll think you're a gold digger."

"I have enough money to take care of myself. How about you? Does extra butter cream your finances?"

"You're on a slippery slope Miss. Just because I'm frugal doesn't mean I'm cheap or poor. I won't waste my money on jewelry or flowers, but I wouldn't mind paying for your oxygen when you're an old lady suffering from emphysema."

She replied, "Yeah, you're a real romantic."

"There's nothing more romantic than being able to take a breath."

"That's easy for you I guess, since you like blowing out all that hot air."

"So, we disagree on what's important in life; not a deal breaker," Bic stated.

"How about taking me to an Orioles game? They're in town this week."

"Sports?" He uttered as if he was a waiter serving fillet mignon and saying "Here sir, is your meat." "To tell you the truth Marisa, I kind of find sports inane."

"Inane? Hey, bagel boy, maybe you're too lame to appreciate sports."

"Excuse me, but you're talking to a former athlete!" he impressed upon her.

"Really, you? Don't tell me. You are too short for basketball, and I can't see you hurling your body to tackle a 200-pound running back, so I'll guess baseball," she said.

"Nooo. Not baseball. During the 1980s, I was…"

"1980s? Thirty plus years ago?" Marisa interrupted.

"In the 1980s," Bic continued unfazed, "I was on the third string of my college bowling team," he declared.

"Bowling?" she questioned as if to ask if that really qualified as an athletic sport.

Bic justified, "I have a very powerful thumb."

Not taking her seriously, Bic continued his opinion on sports in general. "Spectator sports are a passive approach to live vicariously through the talent of other people who pursue a goal of imaginary victory. It's something that real life doesn't quite provide so cleanly, with such affinity and closure."

Bic paused a moment and then Marisa said, "Don't you think it fits nicely with your whole 'fiction is my reality' philosophy? Look Bic, even though other people are doing all the work, it's fun to try to anticipate the strategy and appreciate the performance. You see when you follow a team for a long time, or even a player, you are not only watching them perform that day in the moment, but also comparing him or the team to prior performances. And once you learn the human-interest story of each player's struggle to play on the elite level, you have a vested interest in cheering the athlete to victory. The spectacular play that defies odds. When seeing a small player on the basketball court get guarded by three opponents but manages to launch a shot from 30 feet out and sink it as the clock expires, it's remarkable. And even though his effort is separate from mine, we witness beauty like viewing a ballet."

Bic asserted, "Isn't it a self-delusion of sorts to live vicariously through athletes? If they win, how is it you feel victorious?"

"I don't feel victorious. I can't say that others don't feel that way. I just root for the home team, because I've been following them for a long time and know the struggle they have gone through to get where they are. It's more like an empathy for a starving kid type of emotion. You may not be related to him, but you would like to see him eat, be healthy and thrive. Hmm. Maybe that's why I'm attracted to you, Bic. Empathy."

Jimmy looked at Rebecca, "That's one lucky son of a gun."

Rebecca replied, "Huh, I don't believe it. He got lucky. Can't say the woman got the better end of that, but she made her own choice, so that's that for her."

Bic lifted the toilet seat and groggily relieved himself with a relaxing exhale. After a minute or so, he flushed then washed his hands. He ran his wet fingers through his jet-black hair steeped in silver roots. He brushed his teeth and returned to the bedroom where Marisa awoke to the sounds of his rummaging.

"Where are my skinny jeans, babe?"

"Ughh. Do you have to wake me at…" She looked at the clock, "5:00 in the morning?"

"Sorry, skinny jeans?"

"I hung them up in the closet where normal people place their clothes."

"Yeah, right, that's the last place I would look. Were you trying to hide them from me?"

Marisa got up and went to the bathroom, "You didn't close the cabinet doors! And there are toothpaste spots on the mirror."

"That's where I keep my toothpaste spots. Do you want to sleep with a man or a maid?"

"How about a man who can clean up after himself?" she offered.

"Yeah, I'm a creative artist. I have needs," he said.

"Obviously. Did you have to bone me for an hour last night?"

"Hey, that was love making," Bic clarified. "Something wrong with that?"

"That was fucking, not love making," she characterized.

Bic challenged Marisa, "You got an orgasm, didn't you?"

"So, you didn't have to take so long?" she replied.

"I'm 50, not 15," Bic explained.

"At least chronologically," she slipped in.

"You should be grateful that I can even get it up. You know a lot of men become impotent by 40. Of course, the clinical studies don't mention the waist sizes of their wives, but that's another issue."

"I'm not complaining," she denied. "I'm just saying."

Bic interjected, "What? That you don't like how I fawn over you, dedicate my soul to you, and take care of you?"

"I'm just saying, next time I'm gonna be on top."

Bic shrugged helplessly, "Hey, fine with me. You do all the work."

Marisa continued, "And you don't take care of me. We take care of each other."

Bic reacted teasingly, "No." He accused strongly, "You're wrong. When I get an orgasm, I do it for you so you feel like you can make it happen."

Marisa made an animated face of disgust, "Oh you're so full of shit."

Bic resumed an ordinary tone, "What's your day going to be like today? Do you have a session?"

"Of course. My group therapy session will meet at 9:00 am."

Bic's curiosity about her therapy session provoked a question, "What's the circus going to exhibit today?"

In tune with his brand of humor she replied, "I've got a schizophrenic, a paranoid delusional psychotic, a bipolar, a personality disorder, a couple of depressives, some anxieties, one

Asperger's, and a mixed up 30-year-old teacher exhibitionist who lusts after her 14-year-old students." Then an idea occurred to her. "Would you like to join in?"

"Yeah right," Bic initially dismissed but then thought a bit. "Actually, it could give me some good material for my next book."

Then it was Marisa who got serious, "I'm not kidding. You have a condition. It's not as if you don't have anything to share with the group. Maybe you or they will get some benefit out of your participation."

Then just as suddenly, the idea of participating in the group felt repulsive, "I'm not going to immerse myself in your freak show."

"Hey, now you're mocking my profession. Is that what you mean by fawning over me?"

Bic, feeling guilty, back tracked, "I'm kidding. God, can't I mock you without getting ridiculed?"

Marisa wanted more from Bic and complained, "You've been living here for three months and you don't even want to see what I do?"

"I know what counseling is," he declared. "I see a psychiatrist myself and have been to numerous therapists during my younger years. It's no secret. Isn't it confidential anyway?" he asked.

"You would be part of that confidentiality. Come on. It would bring us closer."

Bic acquiesced, "Fine, commandeer my mind; throw me in the asylum with the loonies."

"So if you're coming, get dressed and come down stairs at 8:50 am. My session begins promptly and some of my patients arrive early."

"Yeah, at least I like the commute to your home office downstairs."

"My patients don't mind that I have a home office," she volunteered.

"Yeah, but the crazies know where you live!" he said with resignation.

"I trust all of my patients; none of them have exhibited any violent tendencies. Even the paranoid delusional psychotic is as harmless as a kitten."

"Yeah, that's reassuring. Half of them can't tell reality from their delusions."

"You have troubles in that area too so don't be so critical."

"Fine. Let's get the freak show started."

* * *

The group sat on plain chairs in a circle. Marisa introduced Bic as the new member to the rest of her patients. "Let's hear from our newest member to our group. Please introduce yourself and tell us a little about your affliction."

Bic feigned a smile, "Hello. I'm Bic Penman. I'm here to work out some issues I have with a mental condition. I have Tourette's Syndrome." His arm jerked into his body. "Yeah, like that. See. I have involuntary movements due to this neurological disorder. So if you see my upper torso bend to the side, or my head snap to the left, or see my arms jerk quickly, you'll know it's not me who's making a gesture, rather it's my inability to prevent a sudden motion. There's no cure, just medication to lessen the number of tics I have. So there you go. That's my affliction."

The Asperger's patient blurted out, "I thought you were going to hit me. I saw you make a fist and you went like this," he punched the air.

Marisa directed her hand in Thomas' direction and introduced him, "This is Thomas." He was about Bic's height but only about 20 with a slender physique. He wore a tight t-shirt that hugged his bony ribs. Then the young man spoke for himself without making eye contact, "I'm just Thomas Perkins. I'm just Thomas Perkins."

Bic was taken back a bit by the oddity of Thomas' speech pattern and social awkwardness, "Uh…Thomas. Yeah, sorry about that. I have all different types of tics. I've even named a few. When I make a fist and look like I'm shaking dice, I call that one my 'gambling tic.' When I make a fist and shoot my arm straight into the air, I call it 'Power to the People.' Sometimes my finger will poke out like a gun. That's my 'Quick Draw McGraw tic.'"

Thomas asked, "What's gonna happen if you don't tic no more?" He snapped his fingers next to his head several times, and repeated, "if no one tics no more?"

Bic returned a befuddled look at Thomas, "Huh? I don't understand the question. I do tic because I have Tourette's."

Marisa interjected, "Thomas. Let's focus on asking questions that we can answer. We're not doing hypothetical questions right now."

Thomas snapped his fingers, and repeated, "Not right now. This isn't do whatever you want to school. This isn't do whatever you want to school."

One of the schizophrenics, Terrell, sat on the edge of his seat. He was a large man in his 30s who looked as if he had been a football player in his younger years. But now, his belly overlapped his belt. Terrell chimed in, "Yeah, that Tourette's you gots, that's nuttin', man. You gots no worries. It's nuttin to what goes on in my mind. I got voices in my head all the freakin' time. They's be talkin' smack to me all day long. Tellin' me tings I don't wanna do, but

I gotsta do'em cause they keep talkin' until I do'em."

Bic responded, "Uh, yeah, you must have schizophrenia. I have an inkling of what you're going through, Terrell. The involuntary movements are just the chief symptom of Tourette's. There are a lot of sub-symptoms too."

Carol, one of the depressives, murmured "Like what?" Then she immediately looked down as if ashamed for making others aware of her existence. Carol wore frumpy clothes that concealed her stocky form.

Bic explained, "Like negative intervening thoughts. I have a whole cast of imaginary characters that pop in mind and harass me."

Terrell asked, "Do dey command you ta do tings?"

"No, sometimes it's just like someone I don't care for invading my personal space and pestering me with questions."

"Dat sounds like schizophrenia, man," Terrell said.

"Well, who knows, maybe I have a friendly version of that. The medical community doesn't really know much about Tourette's, just that a cluster of sub-symptoms accompany my movements, like depression, anxiety, attention deficit deficiency, racing thoughts, gastro-intestinal issues, and vertigo. But the uncontrollable internal thoughts range from people annoying me to trying to intimidate me. They threaten me or someone I know. Or, they harm my property, to the point that in my mind I feel I have to talk back to them or even strike out in self-defense only to realize that I'm not poking my imaginary offender's eyes, but rather gouging my own. If it wasn't for the medication, I might have been blind by now."

"You don't seem depressed," Janis, one of the depressives, muttered while biting her fingernail. Janis was a tall, gangly woman with a beak nose that would be envied by the Wizard of Oz's wicked witch of the East. She was a hopeless 30-something who appeared as if attracting the opposite sex would be a life-long challenge. Her face was plain without makeup.

Her hair unimaginatively hung beside the sides of her face.

"I'm not. The sub-symptoms don't all occur at the same time. Some, like vertigo, only happened to me once," Bic clarified.

Janis whined, "I can barely get out of bed. I hate my life and you can only complain about all these things that don't really matter. I think about killing myself every day. Just to get rid of the pain. It's unbearable and you mope about jerky movements."

Bic felt the weight of the annoying disparity amongst the group's issues and temperaments. "Hey, I'm sorry that you're suffering from clinical depression, but it's not a contest whose affliction is worse. Though to debate about it, I think having difficulty discerning reality from unwanted mental images is kind of important. You know, it's like I can't always trust that I'm in control of my perceptions or behavior. You could go on meds, you know. There are a dozen different anti-depressive medications. Why aren't you doing anything about it?"

Janis responded, "I hate pills. They don't make me feel right, like I could never love anyone."

Bic shelved his sarcastic temptation to point out that sexual intercourse was nothing more than a remote probability for her anyway. Instead, an unusual current of maturity swelled in him and offered a more reasonable perspective. Bic challenged, "So you would rather face death than live without feeling a sex drive?"

Marisa brought balance to the session, "No judgments here, Bic. We are all peers who have something to contribute."

Don, who suffered from delusions, spoke up with a nervous, rapid speech pattern. "I can relate man to both of you. I mean, I can't trust myself when I'm not taking meds. I could go off the deep end, ya know? I mean, I end up believing in devils and such who keep coming into my mind. I might end up killing someone innocent, just 'cause I see'em as the devil. Sometimes I think I am the only one who could save the world from demons. That it is my job.

So, it's like, I might end up, like, taking somebody's life. I don't want to sit in a psych ward for the rest of my life. But the meds, they take me down, like 'Mike Tyson knocked out down.' You know, I hate that hazy way you are when taking meds. To just be, but in a daze. At least when I'm psychotic, I like goes about with a purpose."

Marisa tried to bring clarity to the issue, "Look, medication may have negative side effects, but at least it enables you to live a fairly normal life. If you're lethargic, you can take more rests during the day."

Then Bic chimed in, "My sex drive was diminished for 10 years while I took various medications. But then I came across a new drug that didn't have that side effect. And yes, it makes a big difference, not to be in a haze or unmotivated, but the alternative is no better."

Thomas asked, "What's gonna happen if no one sees reality?"

"Focus Thomas. We are all learning about Bic's unique condition." Marisa said to him.

Bic continued, "Besides, new medications hit the market every year. Maybe you just need to try a different drug. Or, there may be a new treatment not to mention a cure on the horizon."

Don offered a pessimistic view, "The day they cure schizophrenia or depression is the day."

"The day for what?" Bic asked, "When you decide to start living? That day may be way off in the future so you might as well start your living now. Because by the time a cure comes around, your days on earth may be numbered."

Janis replied, "Gee thanks, that makes me feel hopeless for the future."

Tippy, a petit girl of just 19 who suffers from anxiety spoke up, "Look, first you say maybe a new drug is on the horizon. Next thing you say is 'Don't count on a cure anytime soon.' You're talking out of both sides of your mouth." Tippy brought her knees to her chest and wrapped her arms around her legs for security.

Rather than get into a pissing match with the young girl, or even admit that he did contradict himself, Bic simply tried to get at the heart of his point. "I'm just saying, you might as well start dealing with whatever afflicts you now as opposed to a possible medical intervention when you're an old lady."

Janis offered more fatalism, "That just makes me want to give up now. Why wait for nothing?"

"I got news for you honey," Bic declared, "Even if we were all normal, our days are numbered and frankly nothing we do is terribly important. We're all here temporarily. So, whatever meaning you want out of life, it's your responsibility to make it happen while you have the chance, impaired or not."

"But it's just too hard," Janis said.

Bic reflexively pitched back, "What's hard is living without making any attempt to change things for the better, or at least accept your limitations and appreciate what you got."

"That's easy for you to say. You care, you have passion," Darin, the manic depressive finally said.

"I make my own passion. Don't you see? Passion is a byproduct of caring about something that in the end doesn't really matter anyway, at least not in the long run. We all die, and our offspring and siblings die, and our friends, even institutions go by the wayside over time. And eventually, even if you are the President of the United States of America, the memories of you fade over time until you become a footnote and then forgotten. In fact, I will give you 10 bucks right now if you can name me the former Secretary of State under Jimmy Carter."

"Who's Jimmy Carter?" Darin, who is only 20 years old, innocently asked?

"Are you kidding me?" Bic sounded dumbfounded. "You see. That's my point. Forgotten. Or in your case never learned. Anyway, it's all the same. No matter how important you are during your life, few people are remembered. And frankly, even being remembered is somewhat of a moot point once you're dead. I would much rather make my mark while I'm alive. But that's hard to do. And if you manage to overcome personal limitations, financial obstacles, competition, and make a mark on society, well then, great — you win."

Terrell asked, "Win what, man?"

"Exactly," Bic replied mysteriously.

Marissa offered, "I guess not having to suffer like so many other people do. And with faith we can create a happy life."

Bic couldn't contain himself and replied, "The day I substitute reality for self-delusion, is the day I truly die. I'd rather be unhappy and real than artificially happy."

Marisa asked, "Why is that? Why is it so important to you to know anything? Why can't you suspend your beliefs in favor of a comforting alternative?"

"Because, believing in Santa Claus only works for so long," Bic said. "At some point the truth comes around. At some point you ask yourself, how does an enormously obese man fit through the chimney? How does Santa get into the homes that don't have chimneys? Do Santa-made products use lead-free paint? You know, your intellect protrudes no matter what, somehow your instinct kicks you in the rear and tells you, you better ask the questions that will let you know what is real and what isn't."

Don raised his chin and scratched his throat as he asked, "So is that what you do when your imaginary people make you feel you are in an unreal situation?"

"No," Bic admitted. "If I was aware that I was in an unreal situation, I wouldn't bother to react to the voices and images. I would be able to detect that the sensation of the hand pickpocketing me isn't real and I wouldn't turnaround in a panic only to discover no one is around me. I wouldn't poke the air thinking I am poking someone who is obnoxiously leaning into my personal space trying to intimidate me."

Marisa asked, "Why would you poke someone in the face even in retaliation? Why not ask your imagined foe to get out of your personal space?"

"You don't understand, these types of thoughts enter my mind like wind currents all day long. They sneak into my mind without warning. If it only happened once, maybe I would react politely. But when people, strangers, are taunting you constantly, it's more than irritating. It's emotional abuse, and anyone who has any dignity would take matters into their own hands and tell them to jump off a bridge with a finger in their eye to boot. But since no one is actually there, I end up poking the air or my own eye for whatever cross-neural reason there is.   After the hundredth time someone messes with you, you are going to want to kick some ass. It's a matter of an accumulated affect. The first time someone shouts in your ear, you question the stability of that person. You may even assume the person has an abnormality that's deserving of aid or consultation. But after 20 times, 100 times, a 1,000 times, the hell with the other person, just stop screaming in my ear. Fortunately, my imaginary taunters fade soon after they appear. So, most of the time, I don't get swept into my mind's eye. They aren't vivid enough to capture my full attention, and my awareness returns to the point where I can simply dismiss the fantasy. But that only happens for a while; at some point, the 50th or so intervention of taunters eludes detection and becomes the perceived reality without other context so that I am in that moment dealing with that irritating situation. When that occurs, and I am excessively anxious, angry and or fatigued, anything can happen. It's the perfect storm scenario. Under rare circumstances, when I happen to be weakened by life's anxious days coupled with my condition and other reasons to be overall angry, I could explode."

Don folded his arms in a tight grip across his chest, then interjected, "You sure you're not schizophrenic? Man, it sounds like you do."

Bic reflected, "Maybe. The medical community doesn't know enough about the condition to say. Labels like 'schizophrenia' are terms that carry a meaning not only based on someone's symptoms but also by the way the word is defined. For all I know, the definition of schizophrenia will become a spectrum like Asperger's syndrome becoming part of the autism spectrum. Maybe there will be a schizophrenia spectrum and Tourette's will be on one end and someone suffering from delusions, hallucinations, and commands will be on the other end."

Marisa said, "Look, we could all be defined by our symptoms or we can treat them."

Darin the manic depressive admitted, "My condition takes me over. It's like my Dr. Jeckle/Mr. Hyde situation. I don't know when the beast will come out and do things that I wouldn't really do. Ya know what I mean?"

Marisa reassured, "That's where recognizing your triggers come into play. Then it is a matter of anticipation and modifying how you approach similar situations."

Then Bic was compelled to say something to lighten the mood, "Instead of Hyde and Jeckle; you would be more like Heckle and Jeckle."

"Who?" Darin asked.

Bic explained, "The two animated crows. Never mind. I mean a kinder version of your extreme dichotomy. We all have a type of duality."

"What about me, what am I? I'm not that. I am just Thomas Perkins."

Bic reassured, "Right, you're just Thomas. Good thing too." Bic pointed at him with jocular approval.

Marisa glanced up at the wall clock, "It looks like the time for our session is coming to the top of the hour. Does anyone have any closing thoughts or issues that they want advice on?"

Thomas asked, "What's gonna happen if no one has any symptoms?"

Bic entertained the question, "We all have symptoms; that's what makes us human and not androids."

"What's gonna happen if we are all androids?" Thomas asked.

Marisa interjected, "Okay, we'll discuss that next time, Thomas."

Thomas continued, "What's gonna happen if everyone died?"

"Next time Thomas," Marisa closed the session.

* * *

Exhausted from the disclosure of the inner workings of his aberrant mind, Bic searched for consolation, "Was I helpful?"

Sensing his discomfort, she responded, "Are we having fun yet?"

"Yeah, lots of fun putting microscopic attention on the thing that disrupts my life the most and sharing it with the world," Bic said.

Marisa replied, "I hardly call my small session of patients the world. Besides it's all confidential."

"Yeah, right. They are probably gossiping about the new guy right now to whomever."

"I thought you don't care what other people think."

"I don't. I just disagree that it's confidential."

"You're sensitive about your condition, aren't you?" Marisa asked him.

"I really don't give a rat's behind. It is what it is. I don't care. I just take my meds and go on. If other people have to stare when I tic, that's their problem. I'm probably being just as obnoxious staring back at them evaluating their physique, their pot bellies, the curvature of their ass, detecting man boobs, or a woman's cleavage. But what can I say? The human figure intrigues me."

"So when you boorishly leer at a woman's ass, you do so out of aesthetic appreciation?"

Bic denied this flatly, "No, of course not. I do that out of glutinous lust. I was referring to the man boobs and pot bellies."

Marisa empathized, "The aging process can be quite cruel to some."

"Hey, if you take care of yourself, you'll live forever — especially with a head transplant and a great novel for the ages."

Chapter 8: A Stream of Consciousness; A Writing Technique

At night's end, Bic said to Marisa, "Well, your colorful characters from the session have sparked some ideas I can work into my novel, so I've got to tend to writing them down before they fade."

She looked at him with disappointment, "So you will be writing all night again?"

"Just until I run out of words," he replied.

"That will never happen. You have an endless supply of misguided thoughts," she mocked.

"Well let's hope some of those thoughts lead to something someone else wants to read."

She sensed his vulnerability, "Or what?"

"Or, I bomb and my book will go by way of the remainder bin, a slow and painful literary death."

Marisa unbuttoned her shirt and tossed it on an armchair. He gazed upon her as she walked into her bedroom wearing just pants and a bra. She closed the window shades, then asked "So how did you like bearing your soul to the group?"

Bic took a second to consider his response, "Nobody exactly shared much, at least, explicitly. That left me with my own observations of their mannerisms. The group shared nothing personal with me other than their psychological disorders."

"Exactly. That's the purpose of group therapy — to reveal our differences to see how much we're alike," she said.

Unconvinced of the benefits, Bic said, "Uh, yeah. If you're saying I share some bond with people who I have nothing in common with simply because I have a genetic condition, I agree. But why's that important and what does group therapy do for me?"

Marisa entered the bathroom and removed her pants, then hung them on the towel bar. "Doesn't the sharing and the talking help you understand yourself in a deeper way?"

"Uh, I'm going to say no on that one," Bic said dismissively. "I think I knew my condition in a realistic way long before I met this circus crowd."

"But they're just like you."

"They are nothing like me. That's why it took me a half hour to explain my disorder so that even those doorknobs could understand it. It's not as if I am unfamiliar with mental disorders. I have met others who have mental problems. Heck, I've even dated a number of them. I am intimately aware of what it's like to live with a manic depressive. I suffered through all the unreasonable outbursts. Though I truly don't see how talking to a bipolar patient in the "lab" so to speak amounts to much. After all, none of your patients other than the autistic kid, exhibited any symptoms of their condition. We're just talking about our conditions, not demonstrating them. Group therapy doesn't put them in real-life situations that challenge them."

Marisa started brushing her teeth, spat, and said with a mouth dripping with toothpaste, "Well 'talk therapy' has helped a lot of people who haven't come to grips with their afflictions." She swished some fresh water in her mouth and spat again into the sink.

Bic admired Marisa's figure as she pushed her way past him back into the bedroom. Bic gently rebutted her spiel, "No doubt for some people who are unaware, that's fine. But I assure you, after 10 years living with Tourette's, I am acutely aware of my struggles and limitations."

Marisa tired of Bic's confidence. "Well, aren't you all knowing?"

"Hey, I can't help it if I know myself to the point where I can't con myself into thinking that talking to strangers about my affliction, as you say, will help me reach a higher level of self-awareness. Give me medication any day of the week. Do you really think talking about a condition will help a biologically based abnormality? If that's true, why don't oncologists tell their cancer patients to join a talk therapy group and skip the chemo? Really, how much have you conned yourself into thinking that talk therapy is the panacea for all things, even those things that have nothing to do with feelings and everything to do with biology?"

Marisa took offense, "Are you mocking my profession again? First my religion and now my practice."

"No. Psychology is great, Marisa. It just doesn't start and stop at personal disclosure. When the para science of psychology merges more with physiological sciences, then let me know and I'll listen. Thoughts and feelings at some level correspond to physical matter on the molecular level. Neurons send signals and the thought transpires. Change the way the brain behaves, then you might make progress in stopping the abnormal hallucinations of the schizophrenic and possibly treating so many other neurologically different people."

"That's what I'm doing in my own way Bic." She continued, "Behavior corresponds with our chemical statuses. Change behavior and the chemical imbalances can change too."

Unfazed, Bic dismissed her, "Yeah that's what you would like to believe. Tell that to my uncontrollable tics. Perform that 1950s behavioral theory all you like. I'm still gonna tic."

"Would you at all be less of a jackass if there was a pill that would cure your condition? I'm going to bed."

"I would join you, but I don't want to sleep with a pill."

"Jackass," she slammed the bedroom door in his face.

He yelled back through the door, "I'll be in the office writing my theory of everything."

Bic turned on his desktop computer and reclined to induce a state of rumination. He let his thoughts drift in and out of his mind. Should he just be grateful that he wasn't standing on the street corner holding a cardboard sign: "Please help. Lost job, have kids. Homeless. Please give. God Bless." — Hoping the hours in the sun holding that pitiful sign will make someone dig out a few bills, lower their car window and reach out to him so the working fellow can feel they did a good deed for someone down and out.

He glanced at the poor outcasts and wondered why they weren't putting this amount of time and effort into getting a quick job. But that was him. He had never been friends with a sidewalk as a bed nor a flattened cardboard box as a sheet cover. So here he was just like most people stuck in the middle, neither rich nor poor, wondering what real difference does any of it matter. He supposed he was rich by the world standards. Having been born in one of the wealthiest countries — and raised in an upper-middle class home, helped.

Compared to a refugee in Syria, he was pretty well off. But in the end, the relative comfort is a negligible consolation prize. Had he not suffered enough to know how good he had it? Did he need to feel something awful to know he was okay where he was now? He supposed no matter how much wealth, power, or love one had, after the feelings settled to normalcy, the questions remained, and the world was too big for him to change. He could give a twenty to a vagabond but millions just like him remained.

His work was nothing less than a massive chunk of his life dedicated to a meaningless experience. Yet he was not unique in this situation. How many people have no work satisfaction? How many of our jobs were truly useless? Come on, doormen? Even cashiers were being replaced by self-checkout stations. And soon the robotics revolution will become mainstream with an android in every home and ubiquitous, doing many jobs that will no longer be available for the common person. Restaurant staff, no need, when a touch screen at the table could enable patrons to electronically order their meals. Chauffeurs, self-driving taxis. It will be a tsunami of shock when the application of artificial intelligence gets to a critical mass. Only the jobs requiring the most education, creativity, or skill will remain. That will affect the work force for sure, though he supposed that may mean a redistribution of how the dollar will be paid out.

To commit suicide was the ultimate quit. The complete face off with eternity. The one you won or lost as soon as you decided to do it. Who took life that seriously? College students, that was who. They think the grades define their self-worth. If they only knew that so much of those grades were decided before they even took that accumulative final exam. The teachers had already decided whether you'll be an accomplished A student or an average C student, or a failure as an F student. In the student's mind, the grade determined their standing in life. They think it will determine their job, their wealth, and status. Little do they know that most students get either average grades or graduate from an average school. Besides, most employers don't even bother checking grades. The only thing that has any influence was perhaps the degree and the major. Only the elite employers that seek the brightest and best care about which school you attended. The rest of the employers only care whether you have a degree. And frankly once you have a few years of professional experience, most employers don't even verify that you graduated from a college.

As the late hours of the night kissed the early morning hours, Bic's fingers flutter-tapped the keyboard of his computer producing a literary tapestry of thoughts. His writings cartwheeled with a youthful energy throughout the night, perked up by a large mug of coffee. He microwaved the mug every twenty minutes to sustain his acumen, while Marisa and the rest of the normal population slept. His back sank into a curve with a crick in his neck that jutted out so he could eyeball his screen until dawn seeped through the window blinds.

It was time for a break. Or maybe time to crash. He had emptied his mind of nocturnal thoughts. Bic listened to his meandering thoughts as if he was listening to a storyteller. He was somehow at the mercy of the thoughts that entered his brain as if they had a will of their own. Was he responsible for his thoughts or were they the by-product of something else? Could he take credit for the ideas that popped into mind? Or was it all random? Maybe a little of both. No matter, his brain may not be the Cadillac, but it was definitely the chauffeur. He was born with a predisposition, yes, a gift to write. But it was his cognizance that guided this ability to any meaningful output. He drove these thoughts from a nebulous current in his mind to their destiny in print, where they could be showcased for the world long after the winds blew away the dust of his remains. Bic slumped closer to his keyboard until it became his resting spot for a deep, deserved sleep.

For most people, breakfast meant eggs, toast, and the morning news on the ipad over a brew of freshly ground beans. It was a Sunday and that was typically a day to address minor maintenance needs around the house and tend to the bush pruning and edge trimming. But this was no ordinary Sunday for when Bic arose from his blackout from the all-night affair with his love of the written word, he would realize it was the early afternoon. No matter, time was relative, and he felt he spent his time on a worthwhile cause, the meaning of his existence.

Bic rose to a strip of sun that shone through the open blinds and illuminated his closed eyelids. He shielded his eyes as they opened to a squint. He stumbled, still in yesterday's rumpled clothes, to the bathroom…seeing Marisa still in bed.

Bic looked at her lying on her back, "I know I had a long night, but you?" He entered the bathroom and alleviated himself. "Hey, are you up? Marisa, I said…. Why are you still in bed? I thought I was the reckless one who can only think when dew is forming." He walked out of the bathroom and closer to the bed. "Hey, sleepy girl. Wake the hell up."

She lay motionless. He approached with a suspicious curiosity that preempted reasonable fear. He peered at her. "Hey Marisa!" he yelled, then shook her to realize she was rigid and unnaturally cold to the touch.

CHAPTER 9: WHERE WERE YOU AT 3:00 AM LAST NIGHT?

Bic waited, sitting on a metal chair next to a small, square table. He sat in a defeated, exhausted manner with his buttocks resting on the edge of the seat. His eyes stared outwardly in a stark void. A plain-clothed police officer entered the interrogation room with a pad and pencil. He casually introduced himself, "Mr. Penman, I am Officer Smith." Bic felt as ordinary as the officer's name and as empty as the officer's pad. Officer Smith sat across from Bic and looked expectantly at him, then asked simply, "So, Mr. Penman, why are we here?"

Bic looked at him tiredly, "Apparently you need my statement, though I'm not sure what I can tell you that I didn't already tell the 911 dispatcher."

Officer Smith answered politely with a calm authority, "Maybe there are some details you left out. It's standard operating procedure to get a statement in person from all material witnesses. Tell me again what happened."

Bic raised his brow at the implication, "I didn't actually witness much, other than I walked into the bedroom and noticed Marisa was not responding to me when I called her name. So, I went over to her and realized she was dead. I held her hand and it was cold, lifeless."

"Lifeless," Officer Smith echoed subtly. "And how did she come to be that way, Mr. Penman?"

Bic shrugged instinctively, "I don't know." He looked puzzled, looked up to the officer, "Heart attack?"

"At age 46?" The officer shook his head. "That's really rare. And Marisa did not have a heart condition."

Feeling frustration, Bic questioned the officer, "Well, haven't you guys done an autopsy yet?"

Officer Smith felt Bic's suggestion gave him a perfect segue to apply more pressure and clarified, "The body is undergoing a thorough examination as we speak." Officer Smith lowered his chin toward Bic in a subliminal way to pressure Bic and said, "So now is the time to speak up on what happened."

Bic exhaled a snort in defeat, "I would tell you something if I knew anything, but I don't."

The officer was convinced otherwise and began to press Bic. "Come on Mr. Penman, you were the last one to see her alive and now she's dead. What happened? Did you have a fight with her and things got out of hand? As you probably know from all those crime shows on TV, accidents do happen between couples that dearly love each other. It's called a crime of passion. Is that what happened?"

Bic's face soured a bit at the suggestion of a violent domestic altercation, but innocently served up a variant scenario that did him no good. "We had a disagreement last night, but neither of us was angry and nothing got out of hand. As I said, Marisa went to sleep and I worked all night in the adjacent room until I fell asleep on my keyboard."

"Do you hear your alibi Mr. Penman? Do you really think that your story is believable?" Officer Smith escalated the pressure. "You worked all night in the room right next to a woman who is killed without your knowledge?"

After another guttural exhale of disapproval, Bic questioned, "Who says she got killed anyway? She probably had a heart attack or something. That's just…."

"An act of God?" the officer interjected.

Bic snorted in disbelief again, "Well, I mean you can express it anyway you want, but yeah, in that maybe it was her time to go."

"You know Mr. Penman, the precinct has interviewed quite a few people in Marisa's social circle. Word has it you aren't exactly the God-fearing type. Isn't that true?"

"Well, I mean you know, natural causes," Bic feigned a slight smile.

"Funny that you would use the words of a religious person when everyone I've spoken to says you don't even believe in morality."

Bic objected, "I didn't actually say God did it, did I? That's what you said. Besides I find the term "morality" to be a word loaded with implied value judgments. I prefer to use the word "ethical." I believe in ethical behavior."

"Is murder ethical, Mr. Penman?"

"Not typically," Bic said reflexively as a habit of intellectually splitting hairs.

"You mean to tell me that killing someone is ethical sometimes?" the officer questioned.

Bic got more entangled in his semantics, "I suppose it depends on the circumstances. Like…" Bic reflected, "Like during combat in a war, self-defense, euthanasia, abortion, etc."

"That's very interesting," the officer said, "So in your mind, you can be justified in killing another person. Were you defending yourself last night?"

"No. Like I said, we just disagreed with each other. And I'm in no way saying that I killed her in any way."

"Okay Mr. Penman. Wait here." The officer got up with notepad in hand.

Sensing the inevitable, Bic interjected, "I hope you aren't just jumping to conclusions. You know, you are doing your due diligence aren't you?"

Officer dismissed Bic's question and said, "Wait here."

"For how long. I got to get going. I have to talk to Marisa's family and friends."

"Not right now. For now, consider this your home."

"But I didn't do anything."

The officer exited the little room leaving Bic surrounded by white-painted cinderblock walls. Bic sat slumped in the chair and shut his eyes trying to take in his loss of Marisa and tried to make sense of this surreal situation. Someone he knew and had been intimate with, gone, never to exist again. It was unexpected. It was a shock. She is gone permanently. Taken from the prime of her life. Where was God in all of this? And eventually, when it is his time, Bic too will be gone. He sat dejected by everything.

A new man entered the interrogation room. He was middle aged, tall, and thin. His metal-rimmed glasses reinforced his image as a scholarly type. "Hello, Mr. Penman. I am Dr. Gore. I'm a psychoanalyst for the police department."

"Really. Are you kidding me? For what?" Bic pleaded.

"I've been retained to conduct an interview with you. You don't have to do this of course. You have the right to contact an attorney."

"Why, am I under arrest?"

"Mr. Penman, you are what we call a person of interest."

"So go ahead, let's interview. I have nothing to hide."

"First let me ask you, how did you feel about Marisa? What kind of relationship did you two have?"

"We met three months ago, hit it off, and started sleeping together rather quickly. We were good together."

The doctor clarified, "So you didn't know each other for very long. And now she's dead. How do you explain that?"

"How do I know?" Bic said, "Talk to the pathologist who is conducting the autopsy."

The doctor probed, "Let me ask you, how do you feel about her death?"

"Like everybody else, I'm shocked," Bic declared.

"But how do you feel?"

"Cheated, I guess. We just met a little while ago. Things were going great and now she's dead. She's gone."

"No remorse?"

"Remorse? No, I didn't kill her. I feel grief, loss, frustration."

"Some of Marisa's friends say you had an obsession with death. Is that true?"

"Obsession, no, I have talked about it as an issue of discussion. But not in some crazy way."

"And of morality?"

"You want my opinion about it?"

"How do you feel about morality Mr. Penman?"

"You know, I don't think it's appropriate to ask me about my thought processes. That's personal."

"Personal is what we're trying to do here, Mr. Penman. Why does the question make you feel uncomfortable?"

"I'm afraid that I'll be wrongly persecuted for having an original thought that may be contrary to conventional thinking."

"Is that your way of declaring that morality is nothing you can relate to?"

"Hey, these are just terms, words, with definitions that humankind makes up."

The doctor tried to clarify, "So you don't believe in morality, doing the right thing?"

Bic back treaded, "Okay, Okay I see where this is going, and I don't like it. I can think anything I want to think. This is America, damn it. Ever hear of the First Amendment?"

"But in your case, you have a dead lover to account for. And you're the only one who could have killed her," the doc put it out on the table.

Bic bowed his head and ran his palms over his face in exasperation, then ran his fingers through his hair. Bic tried a different approach, "Look, can't two things happen at the same time? I fell asleep and she died. It happens. I can't be responsible for everyone's health status. If it was her time to go, it was her time." Bic supported his head with his hand gripping his chin and mouth.

"So, you aren't feeling grief right now? You simply accept her gone, forever?"

"I'm grieving. But I'm also trying to explain this thing to you guys. It's hard to shed tears when you're being accused of doing something you didn't do."

"Have you shed a tear, Mr. Penman?"

Taken back Bic said, "Okay not literally. I'm not a crier. Okay, look. People grieve in their own way. Not everyone acts like they're at a stereotypical Greek funeral. So, it looks like you guys are starting to build a case because of my personality and not any actual evidence. Can't someone just die?"

"I don't know the answer to that, but we aim to find out. Have a good day Mr. Penman." The doctor stood up as did Bic, in unison. Officer Smith entered the room and said to Bic, "Mr. Penman. Please sit down. As you know we took your statement very seriously. We did not rush to judgment just because your 46-year-old girlfriend died with you in the next room." The doctor left the room.

"Glad to hear it officer," Bic stated without conviction.

Officer Smith continued gently, "But tell us, Mr. Penman, there was no sign of forced entry into the house, and you were the last person to see her alive as well as the first person to discover her dead. Can you explain how that has come to be?"

Dumbfounded, Bic answered, "No, I can't. People do die on their own."

"Except the autopsy results say differently."

"Yeah?"

"Yeah," Officer Smith echoed mockingly. "The coroner identified signs of trauma to Marisa's neck. He concluded that the Cause of Death was asphyxiation by means of strangulation."

"Then she was murdered!" Bic blurted out.

"Yes, Mr. Penman. She was murdered!" the officer said with a tinge of disgust. "To summarize Mr. Penman, you were Marisa's lover. You argued the night before. You were there all night long but did not hear any other person in the household. You have motive and opportunity."

"Motive? What's my motive? We were each other's soul mate."

Officer Smith challenged that notion, "Come on, you only knew each other for three months, Mr. Penman. With all due respect, you were banging her. That doesn't make you her soul mate."

"No. Not in itself. But the fact that we only were together for three months doesn't define our relationship in any other way either. Why do you describe our relationship in a cheap manner? We packed in a lot of living within those three months," Bic explained.

"Well, that's all over for her now, isn't it? And it looks more and more like it will be over for you too."

Feeling the forces of appearances colliding against equal opposing forces of truth, Bic was sapped of energy, "I think I want to go now."

"That's not an option right now, Mr. Penman."

"Am I under arrest?"

"I'm afraid so. We're going to have to book you, Mr. Penman." The officer realized the irony of the law enforcement nomenclature "book" and that his accused, Mr. Penman wrote books. He tried to contain a smirk that leaked out, then regained his composure. "You will have to be incarcerated until your trial."

"So, I'm guilty before proven innocent? You can't do this. This is crazy. I didn't do anything."

"That's the way our judicial system works."

"I think I'm ready for an attorney," Bic said out of desperation.

"That's your choice. But we can end this right now if you tell me what really happened."

"I don't have any more to say. I've told you everything I know. Have you even investigated this case? You know she had a session with her looney-toon patients that morning."

Officer Smith replied, "We contacted all of her patients. We don't believe any of them had a motive and opportunity. Besides, we heard a mouthful that you were one of those looney toons."

"I was just participating because Marisa asked me to, you know, help her group. I agreed just to get material for my book. I'm a writer. I need personal experiences to develop my ideas."

The officer jumped all over the new information volunteered by Bic in the heat of the moment. "So, is that why you killed Marisa, to see what taking a life was like?"

"I did not kill her!"

The officer shouted back at Bic, "Her name is Marisa."

Now Bic lost his composure, "I know what her fucking name is. I swear. I didn't do anything. I just woke up and she was dead."

"Funny the night she dies, you claim you didn't sleep next to her."

"I do that all the time. I'm a writer. I get inspiration in the wee hours of the night when everything is quiet."

"Then why didn't you hear anything?"

"I must've been asleep when it happened."

"How? If you, Mr. Penman did not commit a crime, how did it happen?" the officer challenged.

"You are depending on me to raise a theory? That's your job, not mine," Bic said defensively.

"Look Mr. Penman. If you're innocent, then something happened while you were in that other room. We don't see it. That leaves you and only you to tell us differently. Tell us where we have gone wrong with this case."

"I told you, her patients are…she treated schizophrenics for God's sake, bipolar patients. What about them?"

"That's all you got, Mr. Penman? Someone else did it because they have a mental illness? You know, you have a mental illness too."

Bic clarified, "I'm not saying mental illness is the cause of someone's act of murder, but it could be. Have you interviewed these guys or not?"

"We have followed through on all leads, Mr. Penman. So far, you are the only morally indifferent, mentally ill, death obsessed suspect who had motive and opportunity."

"Well, you didn't have to be so specific," Bic said resigned.

Then Officer Smith offered some pragmatic advice, "It doesn't look good for you Mr. Penman. Talk to your counsel to see if you can plea this out."

"I'm not confessing to anything I didn't do."

"We didn't think you would."

"I don't see how you can conclude I'm guilty just because circumstances arise and you don't know how they happened. How does that make me guilty?"

That's called circumstantial evidence. And in your case, it's overwhelming. So you'll have a chance to state your defense to a jury of your peers. Then it's up to the jury to decide. We just make the initial call on probability. Don't you think you are the most probable person to have committed this crime?"

"But I know I didn't do it."

The officer questioned the validity of Bic's mental state, "Do you know? What's this condition you have?"

"Tourette's Syndrome?"

"Do you ever act without knowledge of what you're doing?"

"Look, Tourette's is an innocuous condition that at most is annoying to everyone including me."

"Answer the question, Mr. Penman."

"It's basically just a movement disorder. So I tic once in a while, so what?"

"According to our department psychoanalyst, you have negative intervening thoughts. Perhaps one of those thoughts told you to kill Marisa."

"Look, this conversation is over. I want to talk to my lawyer."

"Fine. You will have to do so from behind bars." The officer told Bic to stand up and put his hands behind his back for cuffing.

***

Hours passed. The cell guard was a large, uniformed man with deep-set eyes. He was accompanying a senior, well-dressed man who carried a briefcase. The guard opened Bic's cell. The suited man said, "Hello, Mr. Penman? I'm your legal counsel, Jack Hart. I'm here to gather your testimony of what happened."

"Great. I take it you're the public defender?"

"Yes."

Still in a state of considering practical matters, Bic asked, "Is this going to cost me anything?"

"No, the state pays for my services."

Then Bic delved into this situation as if he was buying a business, "Ever defend a murder suspect?"

"I'm completely qualified to represent you in a court of law."

"Somehow that falls short of answering my question. Not a confidence builder."

"Mr. Penman, if you want the most seasoned defense attorneys, you will have to come up with hundreds of thousands of dollars. Are you prepared to do that Mr. Penman?"

Bic realized he was in no position to treat this situation as if he had unlimited time and resources. He didn't have a staff to research anything, so he acquiesced, "What do you need to know?"

"Just give me your honest account of the events leading up to Marisa's death and what you did immediately afterwards."

"Okay, this crap again." Bic continued explaining how he was sleeping in the adjacent room until 2:00 pm in the afternoon when he awoke and discovered Marisa dead. He explained that he was sleeping at such an odd hour because he had been writing throughout the night until falling asleep on his keyboard at about sunrise.

Mr. Hart explored the details in the hopes of uncovering a revealing point, "What were you writing?"

"A novel."

"About?"

Bic felt frustrated at the question. "Is this relevant?"

"I don't know yet. Just answer the question. We'll see if it's relevant."

"It hadn't defined itself yet. I was just writing through a stream of connected thoughts.

That's how I work. The story evolves as I go along."

"So, writing that led nowhere?

"Not yet. It's part of the creative process."

"You didn't have any outline or ideas for the direction of this effort?"

"I can see where this is going, but I assure you it's a process that works for me. I purposely don't start a writing project with an intention. I let the purpose find me, or I find purpose from how I interpret the story. So what's your strategy? To defend me by my writing approach? Let's get real here."

"Mr. Penman, sometimes the details speak volumes. You never know what could serve as a defense. I have to explore these avenues. The jury needs to know the whole story."

"The whole story had not yet been determined."

"Sounds somewhat passive. Aren't you some advocate of free will as opposed to a deterministic way of life?"

"Who told you that? That quack of a psychoanalyst? I'd like to shove a Rorschach card down his throat."

"Relax Mr. Penman. I'm just exploring glaring differences in the way you will be portrayed with what comes out of your mouth. If you are a believer in free will then why didn't you control the outcome of your book?"

"First of all, I never said I think the world operates through free will. Between you and me, I think everything happens via the laws of physics giving only the appearance of free will. Since we can't calculate the motion and effect of every fucking molecule in reality, we can't possibly be aware of what will happen even though what does happen has no choice in the matter."

"Let's take a different approach to this. Since you seem to be portraying yourself as someone at the mercy of the laws of physics, were you somehow compelled to kill Marisa?"

"I did not kill Marisa, knowingly, unknowingly, or in any way. I just did not have anything to do with her death. I don't get it.

Doesn't there have to be an investigation? She and I had only been together for three months. Did she have any other past boyfriends, lovers, or stalkers in her life? You know, an old boyfriend may have had a key to her place. Did you think of that? Huh?"

"It's possible." Mr. Hart said, "We can certainly explore that line of defense. We just need to create reasonable doubt. Their case against you, while I do admit is convincing, is circumstantial."

With relief Bic said, "Now you're talking like you're on my side."

"I never meant to convey otherwise. But I have to suspect you and treat you as would the prosecution to reveal how you will respond under cross examination. The prosecutor will be grilling you about all this, making connections that suggest you and only you were the perpetrator. Your character, your past words, your belief system will all be used to paint the kind of person that may have committed murder. They will claim you have a temper and through unchecked anger you committed a crime of passion by strangling her in her sleep. By your own testimony, you didn't call 911 until the body had been dead for nearly 8 hours. Was that because of remorse, fear, guilt? Or was it as you say, you were sleeping when most people are mowing their lawns?" The attorney paused.

The attorney continued, "We've got to counter all this odd imagery that the jury will hear. We've got to paint a different picture. One that resonates that you are as befuddled as they and that you could never have done such a heinous act."

"You mean present myself like a marketing ad?"

Mr. Hart said in a resigned manner, "That's the system Bic."

Bic admitted, "I really don't feel comfortable misrepresenting my beliefs and who I am."

"How comfortable will you be sitting in prison for the next 40 years?" Mr. Harts asked rhetorically.

"I don't know, do they have HBO?"

Mr. Hart dismissed Bic's attempt to lighten the mood. "We have a lot of work to do."

Bic looked directly into his lawyer's eyes and tried to grasp some affirmation, "Do you believe me?"

Mr. Hart diverted the issue, "It's not me who has to be persuaded."

In a jail cell, Bic pondered not the existential questions, but rather who would cut his lawn while he was awaiting trial? Not the big questions, but the minutia entered his mind. "My bills, I hope I turned off the stove. I guess I'm going to lose my job. Good riddance. That's no loss. Once I get out of here, I'll get a better job, though I might have some interesting interviews trying to explain this mess. Heck it's just murder; it's not as if I embezzled anything. The real crime in my life has been the meaninglessness of my crappy jobs — writing documents that are required by contract, but that no one reads." Now he felt like his life could be wasted as much as one of those documents. He exists but does not matter.

Bic's thoughts shifted to the practical, "How do I prove a negative? That I did not kill Marisa? Then again, I can't just say that I didn't do it. That's not convincing. It looks like I could've done it and I'm the one going to be trotted out in front of the jury in cuffs and wearing an orange jump suit. Granted I had opportunity, but what motive did I have? I wasn't with her long enough to be insanely jealous or angry with her."

He and counsel met again and after a lot of soul searching, Bic said confidently to Mr. Hart, "The whole angle for passionate rage is just silly. I've had numerous girlfriends in the past. I have never shown any signs of aggression towards any of them."

"That's a start, Mr. Penman." Mr. Hart said supportively. But still using counter arguments to challenge Bic, Mr. Hart suggested, "Then perhaps you had your own personal reasons."

"Like?"

"Like maybe ideological."

"What ideology are you talking about? I don't ascribe to any zealous religion. If anything, I'm the opposite of a religious zealot. I can't stand organized religion. It's all crap to me."

"Precisely," Mr. Hart replied, "you don't believe in any religion and maybe that's your problem."

"So, you want to pin this on me just because I don't believe in organized religion?" Bic questioned.

"You tell me whether that sounds reasonable. You dismiss all sensibilities of faith in a higher power. Maybe you're a narcissist who believes he holds the power to take someone's life. Do you have a sense that you control the world? Any God complexes?"

Bic bit his lower lip. Started to laugh. Then seriously said, "Come on, really? That's what you came up with? Taking someone's life, someone I care about, to prove I have some sort of God-like power?"

Mr. Hart pounced on Bic's response, "You know what? A jury could take your lack of a direct response as evasive. Most innocent people would simply deny it. Why aren't you?"

"Okay, okay. I deny it. What do you want from me?"

"Another thing, Mr. Penman."

"Yeah?"

"You say you were writing all night long."

Bic exhaled with fatigue from the repetition of questions. "Yeah."

"What evidence do you have that you wrote anything?"

"Come on. Just check the damn computer," Bic said with increasing indignation.

"They did, Mr. Penman. Nothing was saved on it."

"That's impossible. I wrote for hours. They are fucking liars. They're manipulating this whole thing just to get a quick bust."

"Fact is, the computer was on a blank page."

Bic reflected back to the fateful night. "Oh shit. Maybe the rainstorm that night cut off the electricity. I guess I didn't save the work," Bic practically mumbled the improbability.

"Your defense is rain?"

"I mean the goddamn lightening."

"So, you're typing for hours and don't once click the save button?"

"I get engrossed in what I'm doing. It's a bad habit. I don't always take time out to do that."

"What were you working on?"

"I don't freakin' know. It just kind went on and on about floating thoughts. It was kind of a comment about modern existentialism."

"You mean the reason for living?"

"Yeah, sort of. I guess."

"A lot about life and death?"

"It's not what it sounds like. You're leading a freak coincidence down the road of fallacious suspicion. It's not uncommon for a writer to write about life and death."

"Yes, but Mr. Penman, we are talking about writing about death in tandem with an actual dead body. See where I'm going with this?"

"Yeah, I know man. I see the blaring parallel that has nothing to do with reality."

"Doesn't it though? Did you kill Marisa out of some sort of crazy experiment, a Roskolnikov moment perhaps?"

"I didn't kill Marisa or anyone else. And if I ever killed someone it wouldn't be just to prove I could."

"Remember Mr. Penman, the prosecution will come after you no differently than I am. Make your mistakes in how you answer these questions here, not in front of the jury."

"Are you kidding me? What about all of the other possibilities that they haven't thoroughly investigated?"

"Well, it's not really up to me. The jury and judge will draw their conclusions and determine your fate."

* * *

From his cell, Bic started thinking about incarceration, "At least I'll have plenty of solitude to ponder what I want and maybe write a novel." Bic spoke to the guard outside his cell, "Hey can I get a laptop or something?"

The guard replied "Where the hell do you think you are? You don't get computer privileges here at the Lorton hotel. No free wi-fi."

"How about a pad and pen?" Bic negotiated.

The guard relaxed with a glint of pity and responded, "I'll put in a request, Mr. Penman."

The following day, Bic was given a pad and pen. He went to work and produced page after page of thoughts. In the cell, there was nothing to do but think. Thinking expanded the boundaries of his cell walls into an abstract landscape of endless rolling hills. A Viking emerged and met a businessman wearing a $500 suit. An odd conversation ensued. The Viking pointed a 10-inch knife at him. The businessman gave him the finger and they vanished. Bic's thoughts floated to the surface, "That's how I'm being treated with all these accusations. Law enforcement people were like Vikings using all of their force to imprison me, but they do so in a time period not their own."

Within three months, Bic had his novel complete with analogies depicting societal institutions as bullies out of touch with the times. It depicted the judicial system as out of date. It depended on unreliable eyewitnesses and judgments about a suspect's integrity by junk science interpretations of bodily behaviors. With the slightest suggestion of anxiety, nervousness, and discomfort, they seem to cling to the notion you are hiding a horrible truth. But who would be comfortable in an interrogation room knowing these police officers want to get a bust while circumstantial matters suggest that you committed murder? Knowing that your fate rested in the hands of these officers and eventually a jury of people who were even less qualified to apply the law, crippled one's faith in anything.

It appeared as if his stay at Lorton had paid off. He made his time more productive than the prison of a wasted life at a boring job.

Another inmate lying on the mattress like a rumpled blanket, spoke back, "Why didn't you just get another job, buddy?"

"Are you kidding, man? All the technical writer jobs are the same. And try to change occupations at my age. I'm at the top of my salary earnings. If I changed fields now, I would be paid the minimum possible. And how would

I convince anybody to hire me for a different field. I don't have relevant education and experience for a different field?"

The inmate, to Bic's surprise, was no low life. He spoke halfway intelligently. "So go into business for yourself," the inmate challenged.

"Easier said than done. If I could raise enough capital in the first place, I would have to be able to live without a stable income for years until the business matured. And what business anyway? The only thing I know is writing. And the book industry is in upheaval from all of the recent changes like Amazon deliveries that can undercut the brick-and-mortar retailers. And ebooks undercut the profits for authors."

"So can't you sell ebooks?"

"Yeah, an ebook saves expenses like printing a physical book, storing it, and shipping it, but how does anyone know it exists without a marketing platform? That costs time and money too. Thousands of ebooks are posted every day, but without a recognizable name, an author gets lost in the plethora of publications."

His cellmate pressed Bic, "So why did you just spend the last three months in jail writing a novel?"

"Because I don't give a rat's ass if it sells. I write not for a return on an investment, but rather to be. That's my purpose in life whether my novels become bestsellers or sit in the remainder bin, whether I'm living in a split-level house or in a 6x6 jail cell."

"But if no one reads your books, then aren't you no better off than those technical documents that no one reads at your job? The only difference that I can tell is that the job pays you and your novels don't."

"Yeah, but when I produce a world and characters from my own mind, I discover my soul."

The large guard lumbered toward Bic's cell with Mr. Hart at his side. "Let's go Mr. Penman. You've been summoned to attend your trial. It's time to face reality." The guard grasped Bic by the arm and led him out of the cell.

Bic reacted, "Hey buddy, hands off my tailored suit. I can hardly say standing trial is facing reality. After all, the prosecution and defense make their cases based on what is most persuasive, not based on anything that necessarily has to do with reality.

The guard replied tritely, "Tell it to the jury. You'll be judged by members of your peers."

"Exactly. That's what I'm afraid of. What makes random citizens my peers? And how is a layman qualified to judge anybody without an expertise in law and the knowledge of the absolute Truth?"

As they escort Bic from the cell, Mr. Hart interjected, "Have some faith, Bic."

Bic Penman dropped his head. "I'm toast."

The guard, the defense attorney, and his client walked out of the penitentiary and boarded the bus. The engine rumbled to a start and the bus exited the grounds on route to Bic Penman's destiny with an ultimate judgment — his fate in the hands of others who were tasked with writing the conclusion of Bic's conflict between the real and the imagined.

The End..Thank God!

What Happened to Marisa?

What really happened to Marisa? In the prime of her life, this vibrant woman was found cold to the touch by her lover, Bic Penman. The pathologist's report determined the cause of death to be homicide. Bic was the last person to see Marisa alive. He claimed he did not hear anyone break in nor witness any foul play while he worked throughout the night in the adjacent room where she died.

Based on the homicide investigator's collection of evidence, including pictures of bruises on Marisa's neck, Bic was not only a person of interest, but the prime suspect. Only he, they concluded, had the opportunity to strangle Marisa to death. The motive? The police hypothesized a domestic dispute erupted out of control, resulting in a crime of passion.

Bic was subsequently charged and incarcerated for the murder of Marisa Bookman, based on overwhelming circumstantial evidence. Yet Bic emphatically denied the accusation. His only defense however, his denial, lacked any evidence, alibi, or facts that convincingly countered the charges. But if Bic didn't do it, who did?

There was no evidence of a break in, yet all the members of Marisa's psychological support group met at her home office. They knew where she lived and could have found a way to copy or steal a key. The group consisted of psychiatric patients with severe conditions such as paranoid delusions, psychosis, and schizophrenia. They were all interviewed and convinced the police of their innocence. However, could one of them have lost control of their perceptions and, in an altered state of mind, committed the homicidal act without having a recollection of it?

Or could it be someone unrelated to Marisa's close circle of friends and patients? Perhaps Crazy Carl, whose post traumatic syndrome from his military days as a grunt in Vietnam triggered a flashback to jungle combat where he could kill his enemy with his bare hands.

Indeed, Crazy Carl awoke in the Starbucks after snoozing in a lounge chair. The crushing noise of the coffee bean grinder set off a flashback to the sounds of rapid machine guns spraying bullets in all directions. Crazy Carl believed he was awakening in Vietnam in the heart of the jungle hiding from the Viet Cong. He saw Marisa at the table with Bic. His first instinct, despite a generation passing since he was actually in combat, was to leap to her and strangle her and then Bic. But the moment passed, and Crazy Carl walked out of the coffee shop in a half state of consciousness that straddled reality and delusion. However, like a good soldier, he hid behind a telephone pole and watched the two from a distance without detection.

Could the robber from Starbucks, who was essentially emasculated by Bic, have felt he had to take revenge on the couple? Perhaps he felt he deserved more than he looted from the register and followed her home to murder her out of anger.

In fact, that was how he felt, incensed and in a rage. How dare these people first ignore his threat and then dismiss him so arrogantly. He will show the bastards. After robbing the Starbucks, he ducked outside the coffee shop and hid behind a telephone pole and watched the front door until the couple emerged. He did follow Marisa home. He was compelled to teach these two a lesson, even if he had to strangle her and her beau with his bare hands. No residential front door could prevent him from picking the lock. He did that routinely. And he did it effortlessly, silently, and without detection, leaving the door wide open, which incidentally made it easy for Crazy Carl to also enter the quiet household in the wee hours of the night.

Just then, Don, the delusional paranoid schizophrenic showed up, thinking that Marisa's brain had been compromised by demonic kittens who caused her to simplify the brains of her patients. Not wanting his brain to be simplified, Don felt compelled to rid the planet of such an evil of humankind, even if he had to do it with his hands, which he believed had the power to neutralize demonic life forms. He approached Marisa's front door, and to his surprise, pushed in the open door then entered her house quietly with the prowess of a cat.

Crazy Carl, not knowing where Marisa was in the house, slipped upstairs and walked into Bic's room and saw him slumped over the keyboard fast asleep.

The Starbucks' robber, crept upstairs also, but had to go to the bathroom to do number two. He cursed himself for eating so many laxatives. He thought they were little chocolates.

Don instinctually went downstairs where Marisa held her group therapy sessions and walked around in the dark looking for demonic kittens. He was certain their eyes glowed orange in the dark and would be easy to detect.

There was no suicide note and the bruises on Marisa's neck suggested someone strangled her. All the police knew was that based on Bic's testimony, the couple had a spat then retired into different rooms. Marisa went to bed. Bic went to the adjacent room to begin writing a manuscript on the computer. Yet no file was saved that corroborated his story. And he was the last known person to report her alive, and the first to discover her dead. He reported her death in the afternoon, when he said he awoke, an astounding eight hours after her time of death.

Although the case rested on circumstantial evidence, any reasonable person would reach the same conclusion as did the police investigators. Bic is guilty. He had opportunity and motive.

If it was a crime of passion, no one will know for sure because there were no witnesses or video. It was the perfect closed-door scenario that eluded knowing the truth, limiting investigators to inference and deduction. But no matter how reasonable a conclusion, ultimately, any conclusion is practically conjecture. So, as promised, let's go behind closed doors and see for ourselves what exactly happened and who did what.

As you remember from your careful reading of **The Writer's Story**, Bic's creativity was flowing without any direction until his eyelids were too heavy to keep open.

Marisa awoke as Bic's head slowly sank to the computer keyboard. She pushed the blankets aside and walked downstairs to refresh her dry throat. She collected a tall glass and grabbed a few ice cubes before filling the glass with peach flavored tea. Marisa always found sucking ice meditative, but always resisted chewing the cubes to avoid a costly dental bill. She squeezed a bit of citrus from a freshly cut lemon and stirred it to her liking then returned to her bed.

Passing her office, she saw her lover slumped over the keyboard. Was she too bitchy the night before? Those types of spats never seem important the next day after a good night's sleep. Yet are they indicative of a relationship that is destined for an early demise? She reflected further. Perhaps they are too individualistic to get along seamlessly. Or maybe they feel so comfortable with each other, they each speak their mind without fear.

With sleep still in her eyes, Marisa returned to her warm bed and her tall glass of peach tea to resume her state of relaxation on this lazy weekend morning. She thought about staying in bed for as long as it took to start the day when Bic would awaken, but she didn't know when he actually had fallen asleep. Had he been sleeping for a while or had he just recently submitted to a deep sleep?

No matter. If he took too long, she would have breakfast alone. For now, she would simply relax with her tea and a good mystery novel. She liked reading. It engaged her mind and transported her out of the immediate reality as does a prayer.

She opened the novel, found her place, then thoughts of Bic intruded again like an obsession. Is he right for her? They are so different, but no one can deny his passion. She tried to weigh the pros and cons. The cons were easy for her. The pros were more intricate. He was perceptive, opinionated, and articulate to express justifications and insights; he was analytical and strong willed; he was engaged in life and embraced it. As these thoughts transpired and dissipated, she reached over to her tall glass and took a sip of her peach tea, then another. A mellow feeling spread throughout her body. She opened her mouth and drew in a cube to suck. It slipped too far down her throat and lodged into her windpipe. Her eyes sprang open in surprise and her heart beat hard. She panicked, desperate to inhale. She felt the air in her lungs thinning then burning. In shear panic, she grabbed her throat hard, trying to dislodge the stubborn cube, but it was too late. She died.

Crazy Carl, the Starbucks' robber, and Don each heard Marisa's desperate gasping, got scared, and high-tailed it out of the house, each trying to squeeze out of the front door at the same time. And eventually, falling over each other, they spilled out of the house. The robber, who conscientiously closed the door back into its locked position, wiped all the prints from the doorknob.

Marisa's hands fell to the side and the ice cube, the perpetrator, melted leaving no evidence to exonerate Marisa's very unfortunate lover, Bic Penman, soon to be a convict known as #81021120.

Part Two

Chapter 10: The Post Card

A postcard arrived in my mailbox today. Typically, nothing but junk mail comes my way given most of my bills and correspondences are sent electronically. So, intrigue overcame me when I read the card: "Dear Cory Schulman: Gaithersburg High School invites you to your class of 2001 20-year reunion this August 21, 2021."

A reunion, I pondered. It reminded me how much time had elapsed. My former classmates and I are twice as old as we were when we graduated. A reunion is supposed to be a cause of reflection, celebration, and remembrance. I threw the postcard into the trash bin.

I remembered my lonesome high school days all too readily. It was hormonally loaded with unfulfilled sexual fantasies, awkward social interactions, and academic lethargy trying to avoid failures more than trying to gain honors.

The next morning, I began the hour plus commute from suburbia to my place of work in the District of Columbia. First, a twenty-minute drive to the Metro station. Then a fifty-minute train ride downtown, followed by a fifteen-minute walk to the office building. My job, after all these post high school years, is a Technical Writer for the Federal Government. At least that was my day job. By night I prided myself as a novelist.

Long ago, to author a book proved you to be an intellectual among a society of struggling literates. But the late 1800s is more than 120 years in the past. Now with self-publishing websites and Amazon postings, anyone can be a "published author." Authorship, the once glamorous vocation, is still romanced by many aspiring writers, even though the million or so books published each year could make for a sizeable landfill. Would-be famous and influential writers get lost in the literary slush pile of competing books.

Indicative of this improbable success, none of my six self-published books have been accepted by a major literary agent, publisher, distributor, or bookstore chain. Trying to find my books for sale is no different than trying to find a particular grain of sand along a beach.

This summation of my accomplishments gave little reason to reconsider going to a class reunion and face all those former students again. I didn't belong amongst the athletes, party goers, or high achieving academics. I thought, who would attend their high school reunion unless they did something back in the day or since then to brag about it?

As I started my day proofing Congressional reports for errors, my concentration was interrupted with memories of high school. A reunion pulls the past to the forefront with an angst of anticipation to revisit it again. A potpourri of conflicting emotions greets us. At best, the memories arise, romanticizing the past. At worst, anxiety about measuring up to how your peers progressed over the years overshadows the celebration.

You can bet, upon meeting someone after 20 years, they will be judging everything about you, everything from how you have aged to the standard questions: What do you do for a living; Are you married; Have kids? What kind of house, car, boat do you have? Prying questions that are designed to sum up your totality as accomplished, distinguished, healthy, rich, influential, highly respected, or the alternative, which is for most people very sadly average.

I hadn't kept up contact with anyone from high school. Most of the students moved out of the state. I remained in Maryland as a native and local. You would think that would be an advantage to maintain ties with others from the same high school. Maybe that is so, but not for the former wallflowers and loners, the spectrum in which I functioned.

Maybe that personality makeup is most suitable for my solitary job as a Technical Writer. I spent hours sitting in a chair lording over my computer screen viewing and comparing records of fact to ensure they were accurate and truthful. To break up the monotony after a few hours statued at my computer, I stretched and took a walk to the break room to heat my lukewarm mug of coffee. The short stroll loosened my aching lower back. But my mind also needed a break. A little meaningless interaction with a co-worker is fine, especially with the young, single pretty females. Despite no chance in hell of getting intimate with any of them given the age disparity, I didn't mind glowing amidst their fashionable appearance and youthful energy. The conversations were brief, predictable, sometimes whiney, complaining about what a boss or another co-worker said.

When I first came onboard to a large employer, I was warned that if you tell one co-worker something, consider the entire office knowing it. That reminded me of high school again. In that, if someone asked another student out on a date during the first period, by the mid-afternoon the entire student body knew about it and was already gossiping.

So, high school once again invaded my consciousness: it doesn't matter which reunion it is. But in my case, it was my 20th since graduating Gaithersburg High School at the age of 18 when "life was just beginning," and "I was entering the real world." At 18 the heart and mind are not only filled with promise, but are ablaze with revolution to change the world, to make a difference, to literally live the life spoken by the class president and famous keynote speakers at graduation.

But now at age 38, I have settled into a profession, perhaps even peaked as far as I knew. Wondering about what I'm going to do with my life was no longer a riddle or surprise. My life was half over and was less about the future, which would likely be more of the same. Does catching up on the past matter? Why not leave the past where it is? Why not focus on what is relevant to today and tomorrow?

Then the pendulum swung the opposite direction. I suppose the reunion doesn't have to be all about me. Maybe no one would be interested in my run-of-the-mill story. Perhaps the true value in a reunion is to see "What did happen to all those people you knew so long ago? Who would marry that socially awkward skin and bones nerd who was captain of the chess team? What ever happened to Renny, the proud band leader who dreamed of making it big on the hard rock stage?" The popular ones: the cheerleaders, the football and baseball players; as well as, the wallflowers, the pregnant girls, the lost ones. How do they live now, would they dare show up? With this perspective, an overwhelming curiosity overcame me.

One complicating issue of course was that I wasn't particularly close to anyone back in the day. But, through osmosis, I did know of other students. Take Judy Macintyre, poor stupid mutt. Her peers encouraged her to drink a mug of beer during the middle of the day in the hallways that were teeming with students. She did, but after gulping a few times, she choked and coughed, as her peers laughed hysterically knowing that the "beer" was a frothy mug of urine. Someone let her know immediately, but the damage was done. Her coughing jag turned to dismay and disgust as she tried to regurgitate what she swallowed. Yeah, I don't see Judy ever living that down. Not even 20 years can pacify such a violation of another human being.

I didn't like high school much at the time. Upon entering my sophomore year, the senior classmates appeared like men with facial hair, and women with full breasts and mature bone structure. I was as close to a blank slate as could be. Academically, I was not on the projectile for becoming a Nobel prize winner, nor a scholar for that matter. I didn't even have a favorite subject. I limped along from year to year as a lazy student who mastered mediocrity. I believe I earned more credit for attendance than for anything I did during class time. That didn't erase the anxiety to answer the question, "What was I going to do with my life?" There was always the military. But after a fleeting second of thought, I dismissed it because, I didn't want to die. There was college, but I was ill-prepared to compete on any serious level. So, community college was my way forward.

For some students, high school was the center of the universe, the defining years of happiness, the transition from one's first facial blemish to one's loss of virginity as the growth spurt takes place. A metamorphosis occurs.

Sexual fantasies invade the mind, domineering the time and attention in all situations, whether in the middle of an exam or a class lecture. The thought of sliding one's hand between a girl's shirt and her naked breast caused arousal numerous times a day.

The feeling of an erection based on a thought is long gone at the age of 38. It takes a lot of actual lovemaking to get one these days. Otherwise, it flops around no differently than an arm that has gone asleep and lost all sensation.

Back then, the need to feel loved was stimulated with the passing of just about any decent looking girl or female faculty member for that matter. There were no age limits, just the sensual sight of red lips and curved hips and the magical secrecy of the bust. But at 38, I calculate I have had sexual intercourse over the past 20 years about 1,000 times at a rate of about once per week. The frequency was much higher during the honeymoon years when my former spouse and I engaged intimately several times a week and sometimes a couple of times per day. But after a thousand times, or there about, you could say, sex has become more perfunctory.

Don't get me wrong, the thousandth orgasm is still nice, it's just not as blushingly influential as the exploding fluids that achieve the body-numbing pleasure of the first orgasm.

Another way of saying it, is that what was important then is not so much a priority now. We change as we conquer the challenges of one period of life; we habituate to some and discover the new. So, if sex was so important then, and not so much now, what is important?

Then there are the mysteries and secrets of life. Many of which are complex and inexplicable like how did matter originate from nothing? Others are more down to earth and solvable, such as who urinated in Judy's beer mug? While at the surface it seems trivial, it is a mystery and a secret that for decades remained unsolved. But it brings attention to many issues. Foremost who did it? The why they did it is fairly evident; a joke designed to humiliate and embarrass. Schadenfreude, in other words, is the motivation. More importantly, we should ask what kind of person would do this, and what came of this person whose character is questionable. Did that person regret his or her actions? Or is this action, symptomatic of a person so full of foibles that no matter what situation or circumstance he is in, he is someone who can't be trusted.

Upon coming home from work, I hauled out the trash bin to the curb for tomorrow's garbage removal. As I clumsily rolled the bin down a few steps to the curb, the cover bounced off exposing the postcard invite. I looked at it anew, and with overwhelming curiosity, picked it out from the top, replaced the lid, and carried the postcard inside, saving it from its demise.

After rescuing the post card from oblivion, I tacked it on my bulletin board in consideration of potentially attending the event at the end of the summer. I approached the bookshelves in my study and looked for my high school yearbook.

It was somewhat buried at the bottom of a stack of forgotten books within the cupboard part of the bookshelf. So, I lifted the stack of books with a minor grunt and slipped out the yearbook, took a cloth to it to clean off the dust, and pilfered the inside pages.

Plenty of pictures of all the big names on campus displayed throughout the book. Young men and women in their physical prime. The football players, the former Trojans, were big guys on campus back then, but for the most part became just big guys, obese and simple minded, working construction or some other predictable slot.

The prettiest gal and the most developed guy always "necked" in front of her locker in the minutes between classes as hallways gorged with the student population streaming past the embraced prurient couple.

As I perused the pictures, some of the images ushered in minor memories of people I knew of. Kim Parlsey was the drama queen back in the day. She got into a minor car accident and the next day relived the tragedy throughout each class until the entire student body was aware of her "near-death experience," which may have required a Band-Aid on her forearm.

The eleventh grade should be a time of acceleration as one contemplates and prepares for SATs and college entrance exams. High School should be a great time for the making of cherished memories, first experiences in romance, driving, and taking studies seriously. Why I crashed and burned during the 11th grade can be attributed to many factors. My puberty was not a sudden and dramatic metamorphosis. It was a slow, undetectable growth. Hairs on my chin and cheek were sparse and as lonesome as my own reclusive personality. I lived in a bubble of my own making.

I was neither gifted with an ease to gab nor fraternized in any meaningful way to either male or female students. Friendships eluded every fiber of my quiet being. Nor did I engage in any of the ritualistic mannerisms that nurtured comradery: cigarette smoking, pill popping, or alcohol consumption, thereby excluding me from the great majority of party goers who were equally as shallow, perhaps more so, but bonded through these cross-cultural means.

However, there were attempts to penetrate these cliques. One time I approached Anthony Balducci, who was a known weed burnout. After a brief discussion, he told me that he could sell me a "dime" of marijuana, dime meaning $10 for a finger length of pot. The next day, I gave him $10, and he gave me a sandwich baggy with a finger's amount of weed. I examined it closely and saw little seedlings and a variety of tiny green stems. I quickly rolled up the baggy of pot and shoved it down the front of my pants for safekeeping. He then gave me some paper rollups, which I would use to roll the marijuana into joints.

All day I was cognizant of my special package buried next to my crotch. I thought about it as I walked and felt the small bag until my obsession became too great to withhold the temptation. Between classes, I ducked into one of the boys' bathrooms. No one occupied any of the stalls, so I pulled out the baggy from my pants and placed it on a countertop near the sinks. I then ripped out one of the papers and laid it on the counter. I pinched a portion of the marijuana and sprinkled it on the paper, then rolled it into a joint and sealed it with a lick of my toungue. My dime of marijuana lay out, exposed for anyone who walked in to see. Not thinking of the consequences, I put the joint between my lips, only to realize I had nothing to light it. Feeling somewhat at a loss and foolish, I put the joint in the plastic baggy, rolled it up, and shoved it back down my pants just as the bathroom door slammed against the wall as a tall teacher bulled his way into the bathroom.

Our eyes met briefly as he passed me and entered a stall. I didn't even have time to perspire or feel shocked, but I knew enough to get the hell out of there fast.

I thought how foolish was I to try to smoke my first joint in a public bathroom. I didn't know whether to feel lucky for escaping suspension or incompetent at trying to become someone I was not.

The pot was eventually never smoked, but was hid in my sock drawer at home, where it sat for about a year before I eventually threw it out.

I was neither a ball handler on a field or court, nor a guitarist or drummer in a loud noise-making band. I was certainly not amongst the elite thinkers and doers, for my grades were not only too poor to expect invitations from a competitive college but threatened to fall short of the requirements to graduate high school.

After prodding from my parents to join some after-school activity, I discovered the chess club had no requirements to participate. So, I went. I knew how the pieces moved but didn't realize how educated the other players were in well-known strategies. One of the chess nerds offered me a game. I lost in a matter of three moves.

I came from a loving and functional family of professionally driven parents. Yet I was alone, self-alienated, invisible, aloof, and functioning in an automated manner as the eleventh grade began inauspiciously.

I dreaded first period History class. As I walked into class and sat at my designated seat, I recognized many of the students from the previous year. They were all students I would consider low lives. A young teenage woman who had been known to have had a couple of abortions already. The weed burnouts. Why was I placed in such a low-level history class? I could see the caliber of students were the least interested in academics. I may have been an underachiever, but I was not dimwitted. My grades were decent the previous year. But somewhere along the line, some bureaucrat determined that I should join the rejects of society: the students who were unlikely to graduate high school.

As I pondered my placement among the degenerates, the crowded classroom began to get rowdy as the teacher was absent five minutes into the onset of class. Soon shouts of insults crisscrossed the room as well as wads of paper thrown about. Desks were shoved and fights about to break out, when the teacher finally ambled in, in an obvious state of inebriation. His intoxication was out shined by his inept effort to quiet the class. One of the students, who was in the midst of becoming a true thug and criminal, challenged Mr. Hanson and stormed out of the class.

Second period was English Literature. I sat in the front row with an unblemished view of the teacher, Mr. Bruster. He bragged to the class that last year he was a Physical Education teacher, but the school was short a faculty member, so he was asked to fill in for the year. He was not even beyond his forties and yet wore dentures. The good thing about sitting in the front row is that it's easy to see the marker board. The bad thing about sitting in the front row is that it's easy to see every pore on your teacher's face. In Mr. Bruster's case, the adhesive he used to glue in his dentures would leak out from his mouth and a blob of denture glue would stick to his lips. So, when he spoke, the little glob of denture glue would latch onto his upper and lower lip and stretch in synchrony with his speech. It wasn't long before I found myself staring at that glob of glue stretching and retracting, which sometimes thrust from his lips in a rain of spittle, that I lost complete attention to what was going on, which was usually nothing imperative anyway. He bluffed his way throughout class, telling war stories of faculty conflicts and other personal self-praiseworthy tales. All the meanwhile, he never administered any exams, vocabulary tests, or homework, leaving us to read any book of our choosing at our own pace. This lack of structure was of course the quicksand for any student who lacks initiative and proactiveness. My attention deficit deficiency was also a perfect storm for getting distracted by the slightest changes in the air currents, let alone a dancing blob of denture glue.

Third period Algebra II was pure agony. Since I nearly failed Algebra I, I was unlikely to succeed in a more advanced version of it, especially with the class led by Mr. Casum, who needed to walk to the side of the marker board after writing anything on it for his massive 450-pound girth eclipsed all portions of the board otherwise. This man's body was as spherical as a giant globe with limbs and a fat cheeked face with large blubbery lips. Despite his competence in illustrating the equations, attention to his physique distracted even the most attentive students. It would be unfair to say that his disgusting appearance was the reason I was also failing. But it didn't help.

Ms. Hitch, known amongst the student body as Ms. Bitch, was a senior-aged spinster, embittered with her battle to ever attract the opposite sex. She was the other history teacher who taught the advanced kids. I only became her student because I had been assigned into the lowest level class reserved for "stupid," uneducable students. After two weeks of lost time with classmates who were on the fringes of society, I finally complained to the principal and lodged for a transfer to a higher-level class. The only available spot was the advanced class, led by the snobby Ms. Hitch who lauded over her students as if they were prized show pigs at a 4-H agricultural fair. The students, to me, didn't seem that smart. They complained about having homework like most students. Was I that much inferior to them? Ms. Hitch thought so and reluctantly admitted me into her class with a complaint that I was already two weeks behind and she made her opinion and prognostication known, that she didn't think I could catch up nor keep up with her class. It seemed my destiny was predetermined.

For fifth period, I had a different fixation. Pretty women, the faculty was no exception. Fantasizing of affairs was just the beginning explanation of a mind completely overtaken by erotic thoughts at intervals of every four seconds. Ms. Weaver fit this description. Though I wondered why a young teacher would wear skintight skirts or low collared shirts that revealed cleavage. Did they crave the attention too? Was it a game to distract our pubescent minds?

So, was there any hope of seeing these loser teachers again? To do what, stare them down as failures who may have done indelible harm to me and countless other students? Tell them off, and point out despite their incompetence, I have succeeded. That their pettiness was in the end no more an influence than a sunburn. At least for me that's what it was, because I stand before you now a college graduate, professional Technical Writer, and aspiring novelist.

Suddenly, a wave of more personal memories ushered into my mind:

Suskia was a pleasant, down to earth student in my homeroom class. I thought she was beautiful, but she didn't flaunt her appearance. She dressed and behaved conservatively. We also shared art class together. She was on track to become a graphic artist, and I too had a passion for art. It was the only class in which I felt comfortable. Although I sat at a large table with several other students, including Suskia, I was reticent for the entire year, satisfied with only snatching glances at Suskia.

Despite her proximity, I could never develop a conversation passed an acknowledgement of her artwork as "Great." The opportunities were lost to inhibition and naiveté. But rediscovering Suskia would be one reason to attend my reunion.

Everyone was acutely aware of Marty Barest, the quarterback. Everyone concealed their contempt for such an arrogant ass throughout his days at high school. It was his growing participation with pranking his peers that made his very presence a nuisance at best and a vitriolic dominance of others at worst. One time he recruited several of his teammates, who supported his every whim like cult followers, and surrounded a volks wagon belonging to one of the nerdier schoolmates. While the vehicle was in the parking lot, the strong young athletes tipped the car on its side. He made the ordinary into a fool, yet his antics were all self-serving to bring clarity and purpose to his own life. He needed to command attention to himself by assuming the lead over his flock of followers while disparaging the ordinary students. Despite a lost soul himself, Marty Barest didn't mind being the King Who Wore No Clothes. But I saw through his nonsense that shrouded his naked truth. On another occasion, he brought his Doberman Pincer to the school grounds to intimidate his peers. The dog's testicles were so large they hung like clackers, perhaps a symbolic pet that overcompensated for an underdeveloped man who had no true convictions.

When all was said and done, why would I want to see anyone like Barest again anyway? But I knew the answer. It wasn't so much about them as it was about me and how I measured up comparatively. I was going to revisit the past in the not-too-distant future. My anxieties were already boiling. I flipped through the pages of the yearbook in search for my image. None could be seen. Do I even care? What I really cared about was the here and now, and while content with the status quo as a citizen, I was at a loss as a creative artist. Despite five novels, nothing resulted. I was as anonymous as during my high school years. I tossed the yearbook to the side.

Six months before the reunion, I was invited to an authors' retreat that was hosted by the nation's leading independent book publishers' company. But to get from my hometown near Washington, DC to my destination in Blue Ridge, Georgia, I had to drive 12 hours. I stayed overnight at a remote lodge deep in the mountainous region.

The following day, I attended lectures hosted by authors who had made their mark on the industry and served to inspire the rest of us. Some mingling occurred, and I noticed my anxiety levels were not causing any hair loss. I wondered why I could function normally at this social engagement while my mind was undergoing a gauntlet of flip-flopping emotions whenever I thought about the upcoming class reunion.

The unnerving return to an age of angst was my answer. I really didn't want to revisit an awkward and failed past. Nor did I want to be reminded of my current state of wallowing. And who were these former colleagues anyway. I didn't like them then. Am I supposed to be impressed with how far they have matured and succeeded in life? While trying to tame my anxieties on my way home, I drove along a winding road through the mountain gorge of the Blue Ridge mountains.

I made sure the radio was turned off, the windshield was clear and that my headlights were on to optimize safety through the fog. Visibility was nearly nil, so I drove slowly along the lonely single lane in and out of mountain ridges as the elevation rose. I drove as cautiously as possible when I passed a curve where the guard rails violently split the width of a car. The metal rail twisted up in a telling manner, but has it been this way for a while or is it evidence of a new accident?

The possibility of a life in the balance compelled me to stop and investigate. I got out and peered over the edge of the mountain into the forestation of the mountainside. A car, maybe a Plymouth Reliant, stood vertically on its front grill about 30 feet below partially wedged between trees. I checked my cell phone, but in the midst of the mountain tops, no service was available. I peered over the edge and believed I could shinny down the incline to the crash site.

After a few unexpected slides, I finally came to the car at rest. Nothing was smoldering. No smell of gasoline, so I approached closer and looked through the side window. The man inside, slumped and bloody. I shouted to him, but he did not respond. I tried the driver's side door handle and miraculously the door opened. I cradled the man's head and checked his neck for a pulse. Nothing. He was limp and dead with blood congealing on his head and nose.

Soon after handling his head, traces of blood transferred to my shirt sleeves. I immediately felt the optics of this may cause me problems with the authorities, but my duty to assist the distressed outweighed those complications. I checked his coat pocket for an id. Mr. Scott Preston, Height 5.8 165 lbs. black hair age 35. A sense of incredulity struck my senses as these facts closely paralleled my own profile. I shared the same physique and approximate age and weight. I felt this unfortunate dead man could have been me. He didn't even make it past middle age and his entire life was snuffed out. If he was successful in whatever he did, he would no longer be able to build on that. And if he was a failure, he no longer had opportunity to change his place in the world. Like me, I thought.

I was alive yet there seemed no end to my failings. No way to change my circumstances as a gifted writer without the industry recognition of a Pulitzer Prize or the gratification of a best seller, or even the glimmer of being well known in the book trade. My books never even made it to the bookshelves of a major book chain. My books were published, yet they sat in warehouse boxes unread.

I looked back at the poor soul who lost his life in a tragic car accident, when a thought flit through my mind. Perhaps if I were in Mr. Preston's situation, my books would sell. Everyone takes interest in dead writers. Maybe I could switch identities with Preston and have the public believe not Mr. Preston dead, but me. As seductive as this thought was to my starving artist soul, I quickly panicked thinking of the consequences and the challenges to get away with it. Preston could easily be identified through his dental records and fingerprints, not to mention his license plates. I would have to take into account all of this. My heart and mind began racing with partial thoughts and a sense of urgency before anyone else drove by to investigate. I figured I had nothing to lose, I was a middle-aged failure anyway. So, with that I quickly plotted my scheme.

I jumped into action. First, I not only had to swap bodies, but also the cars. I stood at the side of his car and rocked it before it toppled over back onto its wheels. Without this happening my entire plan would not have worked. I took this fortunate development as an auspicious sign to proceed. I turned the ignition key, praying it would come to life. The engine roared, probably spared from the trees breaking the fall of the car. The engine was compromised and made sounds of suffering, but it ran.

I pushed Preston's limp body to the passenger's seat and drove his car down the incline weaving between sparse trees until finding the next rung of road. Since the road abutted the side of the mountain, there was no guard rail and I easily drove onto the smooth surface of the asphalt. I ran up the side of the mountain with exhilaration and adrenaline pumping until I reached the busted guard rail and hoisted myself up to the road where my car was parked. I then put my car in drive and aimed it at the busted part of the guard rail. I got out of the car and watched my vehicle slip through the whole and rumble down the mountainside. I followed suit and slid down the mountainside to where my car came to rest, battered by striking tree trunks along the way. Now I raced to Preston and removed his body from his car and put him into mine. I heaved his dead weight inches at a time. I was bloody, dirty, and perspiring profusely. My heart beat at an exhausting rate until I dumped Preston in the driver's side of my now wrecked car. But I had to do more. I was in this neck deep; I could not go back now. I was committed so I thought nothing of my next horrific actions.

I popped open the trunk of my car, where I stored numerous emergency tools and supplies. One of which was a hacksaw. I took a dark green plastic trash bag and the hacksaw and quickly went to work on Preston. This man's identity will not be easily found I swore to myself. I looked at this dead man bruised, bloody, and limp. I repeated to myself, as if I were trying to convince myself that he was no longer a human being — that whatever defines him as a being is gone. He was nothing more than an inert formation of material; frankly bone and flesh. I took several deep breadths wondering why it was so hard to desecrate this once living man. But like I said, I was in this too deep now, it was all or nothing.

I cradled Preston's head once again and felt his hair reminding me that he was once a vital person, alive and grooming himself every morning as he prepared for work. But then I looked at the road with his mangled car and knew I had only minutes to carry out my spontaneous scheme. I clenched my teeth as the teeth of the hacksaw pressed into Preston's neck flesh. Then with a heave, I ran the hacksaw back and forth along his jugular, breaking the arteries, but despite his demise, fresh blood squirted, startling me in a phobic reaction. Blood sprayed onto my face and beaded across my shirt. Preston's blood dripped from my brow into my left eye, but I continued more rigorously cutting back and forth with squinting eyes. The hacksaw met the bone of his neck. I couldn't stop now. I thrust the hacksaw back and forth, faster and faster as it severed Preston's head from his neck. It hung by an inch of stubborn flesh. I grabbed the strip of flesh that still connected Preston's dangling head and ripped through it with the saw. His head fell and bounced off my knee to the ground.

I reached down and picked up Preston's inanimate head as if it were nothing more than a bowling ball and dropped it into the dark green garbage bag. "That's it for his dental records. Now for his fingerprints." I proceeded to sever his wrists and remove his hands then dumped them into the bag as well. I rifled through his pockets and took all identifying information and also dumped them into the bag. After I removed my license plates, I ran back to his car with my bag of damning evidence. I tied the bag tightly and stowed it in the trunk and drove away with an engine that was barely alive.

***

I drove through the night, sweating every time I spotted a passing police vehicle, until getting back to my hometown. Before dawn broke, I arrived about a block away from my house where I parked Preston's mangled car and slipped back to my home. I needed to be unseen. My hands and clothes, even face were still covered with blood. So, under the cloak of the wee hours of the morning, I scurried back to my house and shed my stained clothes then showered. I bagged the bloody clothes and collected many essentials from my home: cash, a suitcase full of clothes, toiletries, and a small army shovel for burying evidence. Then I snuck back to the car and tossed the bag of blood-stained clothes in the trunk on top of the other bag of Preston's body parts. The sky was light as the sun approached daybreak. Although I was cleaned up, I still drove a car that called too much attention to itself and was full of macabre evidence of wrongdoing.

As time ticked by, pressure mounted to dispose both the car and Preston's remains. At some point Preston's family or employer would launch an investigation for a missing person. In addition, the gruesome mess I left behind in my sacrificed car would certainly call for a serious search for whoever butchered the man inside. One of the first things the cops would do is try to trace credit card usage, license plates, and search for any witnesses. I had to not only ditch Preston's car but also hide it or destroy it in another state to slow down any investigation.

As sleep deprived as I was, I continued to drive through the morning until I was out of state. I stole a look in the rearview mirror and witnessed the dark circles under my eyes of a man I could barely recognize. Then it hit me, What the hell am I doing? It's only a matter of time before this entire fiasco implodes and I go away for life. All for what? To gain notoriety and sell books. This was the dumbest idea I have ever had.

I was under no delusions. I was an easy catch. But I figured I had a few days at most before anyone would be seriously looking. I had to get rid of Preston's decapitated head and hands, as well as his car, and do it quickly.

All I could think about was how to get rid of the evidence. Many elaborate, theoretical thoughts came to mind, but in the end, they were all ridiculously impossible from dissolving the bones in acid to throwing them into a melting pot. I didn't have access to these substances or methods. I came to the lucid conclusion that my ideas were farfetched and primarily inspired by Hollywood movies.

Ultimately, I had to go to a sparsely populated area. I drove to a large natural reserve, swung my two garbage bags of evidence over my shoulder, and walked along a hiking path which bifurcated numerous times. I walked with Preston's odorously decaying head and hands and a small army shovel in my dark green bags. Then I heard voices of fellow hikers approaching.

I didn't want any witnesses of me, so I hid behind a thick tree. Their conversation became incrementally louder as they approached. They were carefree and cackling with digs to each other.

"Hey," one said, he stopped walking. "Look." He pointed to where I was. "There's someone there. Hey, you," He called out.

I didn't want them coming out to investigate and seeing my garbage back full of goodies. So, I emerged.

"What are you doing off the path dude? And what's that odor, man?"

I instinctually smiled, "Uh," and just blurted the first thought that came to mind. "I, uh, had to alleviate myself."

"The forest isn't your personal toilet man. There are porta potties at the entrance of the park."

"Yeah, I know, it was an emergency."

One of the hikers' buddies, who was more sympathetic or apathetic to my excuse, interjected, "Common man, let the dude do his business in peace."

"No, it's disgusting. I'm going to report you to the Mountain Ranger."

And like an old married couple, his buddy complained, "Why do you have to be a stickler for the rules all the time?"

In my candid defense, I rebutted, "Not any more disgusting than all of the rabbits and other wildlife pooping there too."

"But human waste is different."

Becoming impatient, the hikers' buddy chided, "Just shut up and let's go."

They left and continued arguing the matter as their voices became distant.

I walked deeper into the forest far away from the path until I could no longer see it. Got out the army shovel and started digging. It didn't take too long to dig a whole that would hold all the body parts, but I dug a little more just in case some animal could smell it and tried to claw it out. So, I dug wider and deeper about three feet. I dumped the human contents from the bags into the hole so they would decompose naturally. I placed the green bag on top of the body parts and shoveled the small mountain of dirt back into the hole to cover everything. I brushed my hands against my pants knowing full well that I looked like I just dug a hole in the forest bed. But I had to take the chance and left.

I took the other bag full of my bloody clothes and buried them along with the shovel about a half mile further into the forest. Then I hurried back to Preston's car and thought about my next move. I needed a roof over my head. I needed privacy.

***

I drove far away looking for a place to abandon Preston's car. The bus depot seemed like a good place, so I parked there and removed the plates to make it a little harder to trace back to Preston. Hopefully, it would sit there for a while then get towed where it would sit more until, with a little luck, get discarded and crushed for recycling. I didn't know whether anyone would bother to check serial numbers against cars reported stolen, or if Preston's car would be reported stolen. I didn't know anything about him. If luck struck, me he wouldn't be missed. But who isn't linked to someone? Family friends, neighbors, co-workers.

At some point, someone is going to say who's seen Preston lately, and try to get in touch with him. And the process starts with tracking his credit, online activity, license plates and so forth. My interest, of course, was for that investigation to never cross with the inevitable investigation of "my own" gruesome butchery. My hope was that the police would think the dismemberment of "my" body parts was mob or drug related. Maybe a serial killer.

As I took a bus to anywhere, I felt completely anonymous. I basically killed myself, or at least my identity. So, what was left: a wandering man with a grand in cash in his pocket. That wouldn't go too far. I had to find work and shelter without identification. That probably meant posing as an illegal worker. Whatever I thought of myself in relation to others, I would now be functioning like an unfortunate person on the fringe of society. A sense of regret came over me, yes, I was somewhat undercover, I wasn't really an undocumented laborer, just a Technical Writer and novelist trying to make some noise in the marketplace.

Not only were the immediate needs pressing me, but it also dawned on me that at some point I would have to reveal all of this to the press. So, I'm kind of screwed either way. I could easily get caught and accused of morbidly killing Preston. Or, if the authorities believed my story, at best get off on probation for mishandling a corpse, failing to report an accident, interfering with police investigations, and theft of Preston's identity. On second thought, despite my clean history, I wouldn't escape all of those charges. I would see some incarceration time. If, by some miracle of police incompetence, I do succeed and avoid detection and capture, I would have to reveal the truth at some point in order to benefit from my deceptions. I think I didn't think this through. Of course, I didn't. It was a spur of the moment, impulsive action. An opportunity that lent itself for exploitation. But I think now, I will have to live the life of a lowlife fugitive — a marginalized, minimum wage, middle-aged laborer.

Looking at this whole mangled mess differently, what if my fly-by-night plan actually pans out? I was basically nothing before this master plan. Now there's a chance the world will take notice. I will write my obituary and submit it to all the major literary outlets. Everybody is intrigued by a dead writer, especially a morbid murder mystery.

From the local library, I scoured the major newspapers and internet stories to see if any information broke from either case, "my decapitated murder" or Preston's missing person, or my greatest fear of an understanding by the authorities that the two cases are interlinked. To my relief, finding nothing, I proceeded to look for houses to share rentals. I assumed I could rent a room far more easily than a commercial rental apartment. Most likely, I could get away with just coming up with the money without needing to prove my identity.

And I was right, after a few miscues, I found a basement room available for $600 per month, utilities included. Just what I needed. Then I walked to the neighborhood shopping center, entered the first establishment I saw, Whiz Car Wash, and asked for a job. The lady, the owner's wife, took care of this matter. She said that she didn't have anything right now in terms of permanent placement, but that I could try my luck just showing up to work at 5 am and wait in line for an opening as the demand for car washes increases throughout the day. Only after chosen by the managers to start work does my time count against the clock. So, I could be waiting for hours for the opportunity to earn minimum wage. I decided that is what I'd do. It's not ideal, but at least I didn't need to prove my identity. They didn't ask many questions, given all their crew members were otherwise unemployed men, many of whom had shady pasts or downright criminal backgrounds.

The next morning, I showed up at the car wash. It was still dark, but the sun would rise soon enough. My eyes had circles around them full of unclaimed sleep. A line of scraggly men sat along a stone wall waiting for the car wash to open. When it did, the owners called forth those men who had seniority, proving to be reliable workers. I waited through sunrise as more and more cars approached.

After five hours of waiting, I was finally chosen as if I were a primary school child getting picked for a kickball game and seeing all the good players picked first. I wouldn't get paid for the five hours of waiting, but I would get paid from 10:00 to 5:00.

As the cars emerged from the car wash, a team of us converged on the car with our hand towels and wiped off the beads of water. One of us entered the car, craned our neck sideways then sprayed the back windshield and rubbed it to a sparkle. We vacuumed under the floor mats and threw down some scented deodorizer packets.

After my day of waiting and working, I estimated that this job would not reliably support myself, so I entered Pizza King and asked for night hours. Like most places of this caliber, they didn't even require an application. Workers changed periodically and expectantly. Whether they were high school kids working part time or grown men who never graduated high school, the longevity of any worker was ephemeral, which gave me the opportunity to slip in. During my teen years, I made pizzas and sandwiches, so all the demands of the job were second nature to me anyway.

Now I had two minimum wage jobs and a dwelling shared with another tenant, Don Prestogeorge, a cartographer just starting to map out his life, but who was directionless. I fit right in.

I had to lay low, be essentially off the grid of detection. Being an aloof person by nature, I didn't know many people anyway. So, the potential for getting identified was slim. Yet I soon developed tendencies of paranoia. I had a lot riding on this. I could get falsely blamed for murder, or at the least, evidence tampering, obstruction of a police investigation. A risk all for promoting my ambitions to become a known author. I didn't guilt myself too much because I know what I'm up against. A million books published every year. Only 60,000 books were accepted in the one last remaining book chain, where most are sold. Amazon is the omnipotent bloodsucker of them all. They peddle books for steep discounts and resell used books for one tenth of the retail price. How can any no name writer such as me emerge from the pack of millions of wannabees? I've joined literary groups, attended county book meetings, even earned an award from a literary contest, I've published articles, and received some press coverage. Yet after 10 years of writing five novels, I barely have sold enough to pay for the printing of my next novel.

But now, essentially on the lam, I've given up my full-time job, since pretending dead involves not showing up anywhere, like to work. I've lost my plush house, and all my belongings, photographs, paintings, my mug collection, books, everything will probably be placed in storage and, after a few months of non-payment, the contents will be auctioned off.

More importantly, I've lost my identity, my car, and my driver's license. I can't use my credit cards or bank savings. I have to start over without my former privileges.

Now I'm relegated to working any job I can get. I am no longer an educated professional writer; I'm a minimum wage laborer washing greasy dishes and sliding pizzas into 500-degree ovens. Or I'm waiting hours for a chance to work wiping down vehicles at the car wash. On top of all that, I must live a life of a liar. In almost all situations, I have to lie about everything, my background, my ambitions, my state of affairs, my education, even my own name, which is no longer Cory Schulman, but rather a pseudonym: Roy C. Luschman, which I birthed from my original name as an anagram. I never did like my name Cory anyway. Strike one advantage for upheaving one's life. But in retrospect, I could have always changed my name without faking a macabre murder.

The hardest part of faking a new identity is keeping up with all the lies. Remembering what you tell people. Making up the back story to explain why a 38-year-old is working at a restaurant and car wash. Either I had a shady background or was a profound loser. I went with the profound loser background, but I spiced it up attributing my lack of ambition to chronic health problems.

I tried not to enter such conversations, but at times they were unavoidable. So, I tried to incorporate some truthful background information to maintain a streak of credibility. Like when Ron, shady background, asked me where I learned how to spin pizzas over my head, I told him the truth that my first job when I was 15 was working for Pappy's Family Pub. Spinning pizzas was required to entertain the audience of 7-year-olds who ran up to where the pizza makers were flipping pizzas and pressed their little grubby hands and snotty noises against the large pane of glass that divided us from them. They studied our motions as we kneaded the dough ball and placed it in the flattening machine. After sprinkling some flower over it, we folded it over our knuckles and gave it a spin, thrusting it up in the air. As it came spinning down, I would punch it up with another twist of the knuckles again and again until the plate sized dough stretched into a large circle the size of a pizza pie. We would flop it over a screen, dunk the ladle into the marinara sauce and, in turn, draw out the sauce in concentric circles on the dough leaving a half inch along the perimeter for the crust to rise. We would grab a fist full of shredded mozzarella and sprinkle it to blanket the red sauce. We placed the toppings then scooped a long pizza spatula under the pizza screen and thrust the pie into the oven where five or so other pizzas were in various states of baking.

Working in anonymity was somewhat ironic in relation to my goal to become famous. For the first time I recognized a shallow streak in my ambition. I always had convinced myself that I wanted to be a highly respected author who wrote books that shook up society and changed the culture in a positive way. To do that however, you must be well known and sell a lot of books that actually have that effect on the reading public. But without breaking through the tsunami of competing published books, I had to resort to extraordinary measures to call attention to myself. Yet here I was seeking as little attention as possible as a mole in the underground. As I doubted my motives, a swell of regret came over me. To get somewhere, I gave up everything to become nothing. That seemed to be the equation and result.

I couldn't come out and confess. I would get thrown in jail for one crime or another. Then the irony of it all fell on me like a ton of books. My plan for media coverage going viral depended on my confession. That was the entire, hair-brained plan in the first place. Yet if I do that and no one cares, I lose even the freedoms I have now. My mind was intertwining as much as a Rubrik's cube made from taffy. I really stepped into this one.

Or maybe I was just reeling from physical and mental exhaustion. After all I had to show up at the car wash by 5:00 am and finished my shift at the pizza parlor by 11:00 pm.

Then, a thought. What if I just started over, which really isn't true either, since I already have an education. I just couldn't use it on an application. But could there be a way to emerge in the ranks of society using the advantages of an education. I may have to resort to a few devious tricks, such as stealing someone else's social security number, but that pales in relation to decapitating a corpse's head. That seemed to be my new moral compass. When in doubt of doing something wrong, I can always rely on that relative relationship: "It isn't as bad as severing the head of a dead body with a hacksaw and lying to the world that you're dead."

I made getting ahead my first order of business. I told the pizza parlor that I could work for them full time if they promoted me to supervisor. I told them, I had worked in this capacity before, and they simply took my word for it without doing any background check. It was very informal. They took me up on the offer which enabled me to quit the car wash given that was eating up most of my time and half the time I wasn't even getting paid while I waited for work to become available. In essence, the future was full of unrealized opportunity.

Chapter 13: In Memory of...

My plan to sensationalize my death in the media, in the hopes that it would stimulate sales of my books, began with me informing on myself. Before contacting anyone, I wrote my obituary, which went like this:

> A decapitated and mutilated corpse believed to be the remains of contemporary Author, Cory Schulman was found last week in his vehicle along Route 60 near Blue Ridge, Georgia last week. Authorities reported that both Schulman's head and hands were missing from the crime scene.
>
> Persons close to Schulman have been interviewed but have not resulted in any leads to the perpetrator of the crime. Although the deceased has no known enemies, the macabre nature of the crime may suggest the involvement of organized criminals, a gang or serial killer. The dismemberment was a likely effort to conceal or delay discovery of the victim's identification. However, the VIN was traced to Schulman, age 38.

Anyone with knowledge of this morbid crime is urged to call their local precinct.

Schulman was best known for his works in fiction, which engaged his readership in profound contemporary issues including faith, marriage, and science. His most notable work, *The Writer's Story*, earned an honorary mention in the *Writer's Digest* general fiction annual awards of 2019. Schulman's books are available through the publisher's website: BestSellerPublications.com

Schulman has no surviving members of his family. His remains will be donated to scientific research as indicated in his will.

After researching all the local and major news outlets, I compiled a list of fax numbers to their editorial staff and newsrooms. I bummed a ride from a fellow pizza maker to get to a local office supply place and faxed my obituary to all the news sources I had listed in the hopes of creating a buzz amongst the public.

The next day, I researched all the independent bookstores I could find and asked them to pay a tribute to a rising, but fallen, star by displaying "his" books. Under the guise of my pseudonym "Roy C. Luschman," I promoted the Schulman sorrow at all the book clubs, writer's meetings, and editor's groups that I could find. After an exhausting promotional effort, I had to lay low a few more weeks to see if anything would come from my diabolical, if not now dysfunctional plan.

For me, success meant nothing less than seeing my books for sale in the largest book retailer in America: Barnes and Nobel. To achieve this end, I collected an array of articles about my lurid "murder" case and sent them to the book chain's head office, accompanied by a letter indicating the huge number of sales that have already occurred to convince them they were missing out on a sales bonanza.

Six weeks later, I contacted a nearby Barnes and Nobel and inquired about my books. The clerk explained, "We haven't stocked them yet, but they're available in our New York stores. I can place an order for you if you like."

I declined the order but wanted to get a more realistic feel for the consumer sales behavior. So, I took a $25 bus ride from D.C. to New York city, which only took a few hours. I walked into the Barnes and Nobel on 5th Avenue and there I was, so to speak. My five books of fiction displayed just as patrons entered the giant retailer. An accomplishment I couldn't do when I was "alive." People were perusing and prodding, reading, and peeping through my books with tentative curiosity. I spied on customers from a distance closely watching their behavior, interacting with my books. How they looked at my books. Were they looking at the cover design, reading the synopsis, leafing through it? For how long did any of my books hold their attention? What if any facial reaction did they offer? And most importantly, did they purchase any?

Soon not only did the *New York Times* write an article, but other major newspapers did too. It seems the story had all the right mix of crime, fame, mystery, and horror to elicit interest from both the press and the public.

But after a spike in sales, the press coverage moved on to other stories. I needed a new plan. I had to fan the flames of my devilish scheme. So, I contacted one of the reporters who wrote an article about my mystery and promised her some details to the crime that only the "true killer" would know.

This intrigued the reporter who listened attentively to my spin on things. We arranged to meet at a local Starbucks where I would reveal some shocking details for her scoop.

Like a blind date, I waited in the lounge of the café and spied the front door, examining every entrant to determine the reporter. Couples came in, a blind person with a service dog entered, even a pack of teenagers invaded the store with boisterous obliviousness to the otherwise tranquil ambience.

I sat considering what exactly I would give up as far as information. Should it be the details of where Preston's head and hands are buried? Or would that just make my plan implode altogether?

I kept watching the doorway, until a young woman carrying a large handbag entered and scanned the lounge. I nodded to her. "Over here."

She came in, extended her hand and introduced herself confidently, "I'm Cherelle Brown, *New York Times* crime beat reporter."

I stood up, shook her hand, stared her in the eye, and simply identified myself as "I'm your contact for the Schulman story."

"No name?" she questioned more as a statement.

"Believe me. You wouldn't want to know. It's to your benefit to know as little about me as possible."

"So, what do you have on the Schulman case?"

I kept digging through all the phases of my riddled project searching for something I could offer that no one else knew about and that hasn't already been revealed by the press. I stalled a bit and asked, "How did you get this assignment anyway Cherelle?"

"Believe me, it's not my only story. So…time is money, sir. What do you have?"

"Okay, okay. Let's just say, Schulman's 'accident' was no accident."

"Obviously, he was dismembered. No one thinks it was accidental. Is that all you got?"

"Putting it another way, it wasn't murder either."

"Then what was the point? He's dead, can we agree on that?" the reporter exasperated.

"Let me give you something substantive." I finally caved realizing I wasn't getting anywhere.

"You have now intrigued me for the first time."

Then I revealed, at a cost of blowing up the entire plan, "You will find the head and hands in the national parklands in Maryland. Just have the police bring canines about a mile into the park; there you will find the remains buried about three feet below the surface about a half mile off the trail at the 87th marker."

"Again, sir. Did you have anything to do with this?"

"Isn't the information good enough for you?"

"I can make it work for me. I just thought I would ask."

She asked several times whether I had anything to do with the crime. I didn't give away any more than a smidgeon of truth, enough only to write another article. When she was done, the next week I repeated the procedure giving her another clue to the puzzle.

It wasn't long before one of my books did make the *New York Times* Best Seller List, which was my goal all along, but now I had to reveal the truth and face the music, which would most certainly be off-key.

As supervisor, I was more integral to the owner's operation. I cemented that relationship with loyal, accurate, and reliable work which was hard to find in a drifter or young student who typically had these types of jobs. I didn't make much more money, only about a dollar more an hour, but the access to employee records was essential to my plan to hijack someone's social security number. While I did my weekly spreadsheets and payroll, I copied numerous employees' identification information if they were available. As I noted, they didn't even perform a background check. It was just a mom-and-pop parlor.

A glimmer of hope arose that I may be able to re-establish myself in some sort of respectable way through devious means of course; but nonetheless, I felt destined to rise in the ranks.

Within two months, I was promoted to Operations Manager and held the keys to open and close the shop. Relations between me and the owner were so good that I could rely on him as a reference to jump into a more professional managerial job in some more lucrative industry.

After having a couple of months of reflection on everything I had done, I regretted it all. I just didn't have the balls to confess, so I was stuck in a life where I had to lie at every turn to conceal my real identity while I struggled to make my new identity meaningful in some way.

Despite my complex and often contradictory feelings, I was at least in a stable place surrounded by the lower classes, but sweet, nonetheless. They embraced me as one of their own linked by near poverty and simple joys of beer and pizza, sports, and music from the old juke box.

The motley crew of ex-cons, losers, and teenagers who performed the shift work became friends through association of the parlor. I knew I would never connect with them on an intellectual level, but on simple things, they were like family. I felt unthreatened and at ease at the low bar I had to climb to be accepted among them. A little snort of cocaine and I was one of them as far as they were concerned. I felt the high immediately and internally was annoyed rather than anything else. It was not my nature to do drugs, but I knew the action would bond me to an endless circle of associates. Occasionally the discussions became somewhat intriguing as John, the owner's son, took a drag from his cigarette, exhaled over his frothy beer mug and calmly bragged that he was 1/16 Cherokee then tried to guilt us all for being the descendants of those who stole his forebearer's land.

I watched over my friends' table from the workstation where I flattened a dough ball and started flipping it into the air then rotating it in circles as I punched and twisted my fist into the expanding circle of dough. I threw it up again into a speedy spin, but it went a little higher than I wanted, and the dough caught the corner of the ceiling air vent, which made the pie ricochet erratically in lateral direction. It finally landed, but on a patron's glistening high heels.

I rushed over to the fashionable woman wearing a tight leather jacket that captured her womanly curves and large bust. Her jacket cinched at her thin waist above her rolling hips and long dancer's legs. She was stylish despite aged beyond a young woman. She asked, "Do you always use the air vents to toss your pies?"

I smiled politely, and embarrassed, scooped up the dough that collapsed onto her undoubtedly expensive shoes and threw it into the trash bin. Then she placed her order: "I'll have a plain medium pie, hold the dirt from the floor," she added to ensure an avoidance of repeating my errant actions.

"Can I have a name for your order?"

"Bookman," she enunciated, glaring into my eyes as if she's known me in a previous life.

Then it was as if lightning struck me, and I came to life. That name: Bookman. How incredible is that? Unbelievable. Astounding. What are the chances of someone actually bearing that name, the same name I used for one of my characters in my previous novel, *The Writer's Story*?

I went back to the sandwich bar and placed her order. I was discombobulated, dumbfounded, and in a tizzy of emotions. I didn't know what to think. Is this some sort of joke? Does she really know my true identity and has come to out me? She's playing with me. That's it. I went through the motions of preparing and boxing pizzas per the orders.

When Bookman's order was ready, I met her again at the cash register to process the transaction. She gave me her credit card and, as I suspected, her first name was Marisa. Just like in my book. She even appeared as stylish as I described her character. But who is she really? And what does she want with me?

"Thanks, Mr.?"

I reply knowingly, "Luschman."

"Luschman?" She said equally knowing that it's a pseudonym. She tortured me by asking, "Where is that name from?"

But I'm prepared for follow up questions and quickly responded, "It's Eastern European." I try to end the conversation so I can think this through, and say, "Thanks for coming in tonight, goodbye. And I turnaround to my work counter.

The next morning, she comes back and calls out to me, "Hi Mr. Luschman," as if we were best of friends. "You work the day shift too?"

"Yeah," I confirm, "60 hours a week usually."

"You have quite the work ethic."

"Is there something I can prepare for you Dr. Bookman," I said knowing her degree from the profession I gave her in my book.

"Call me Marisa. Dr. Bookman is my professional name, I only use at the office."

I don't pry or ask any questions because I was spooked out of my mind. But I felt I must engage with her to know exactly what she wanted. Maybe I can negotiate my way out of this fix.

"What may I call you? Mr. Luschman is too formal for me. I'm a personal woman."

"Roy. Call me Roy, Marisa. What do you want?" I asked bluntly, cutting through the niceties. Really asking her, what does she wants with me?

"If you would care so much as to meet me for coffee someday this week. I have something to discuss with you."

Resigned, I said "Sure, I have a day off on Thursday."

"Meet me at the Rockville Center's Starbucks at noon, won't you?"

"Sure thing. I'll be there Marisa," knowing she is asking me to meet her at the very Starbucks that I featured in my novel. This is definitely no coincidence, and I feel very much in danger.

CHAPTER 15: MARISA

With little to lose, or maybe I should say, with everything to lose, I went to the Rockville Center Starbucks to meet Marisa Bookman. She was there waiting for me.

"On time. Good for you, Roy, or should I call you by your real name, Cory Schulman? Or by that caricature of yourself in *The Writer's Story*, Bic Penman? Could your character names be any less contrived? Penman? Bookman? I thought you considered yourself a creative genius?"

"Alright, so you know who I am. I'm busted. More importantly, who are you and what do you want? You just don't want to critique my writing, do you?"

"What I want depends on you, Cory."

"I'm listening."

"Relax Cory. You haven't even offered to buy me a café latte? You're a clichéd writer, aren't you? So you must drink a lot of coffee."

"I gather you're not a fan of my writings? Have they offended you to the point that you must harass me?"

"In part I am here as a protest to your god-awful themes of anti-religion and anti-marriage bitterness. You know these are concepts that contradict every fiber of my being, given that I'm a psychologist and rabbi."

"So," I shake my head, "If my books are so offensive to your nature, don't buy my books."

"That's not so easy. You created me and left me to die at the end."

"That's fiction. I can do anything I want. In essence when I'm writing, I am god."

"There's that egotistical smart-ass attitude just beneath the surface of your smug little face. Religion and the sanctity of marriage are cornerstones to our civilized society."

My rebuttal, "If organized religion is so essential, why is it some sectors of your religion don't recognize you as a legitimate rabbi given your gender?"

"That is just a technicality and fault of the establishment to embrace what it means to be a true believer."

"Look, uh Marisa, believe in anything you want. That's your prerogative. As is mine. I don't have to succumb to some blind faith in a superbeing, nor do I have to pray. I'm fine just the way I am. So, what are you going to do about that? Kill me? That would be contrary to your belief system, wouldn't it?"

"Even religious people sin Cory."

"So that's the reason you've come to me. To Kill me? Because you didn't like my anti-ritualistic themes in my book? Why don't you just email me a complaint letter like everybody else?"

"You see Cory, I'm not really bound by my religious teachings because I'm not really real. I'm your creation born from your imagination. I can do anything I want. Even take revenge for killing me in your book."

In my defense, I said, "I had to do that to illustrate that bad things can happen to good people, as is the case with my protagonist who goes to jail based on a circumstantial case of murdering you."

"You killed me. You, Cory Schulman, killed me with your poison pen."

"It was an accident, at least in the book. You choked on an ice cube and suffocated to death. The evidence melted, leaving Bic…"

"You mean you."

"I mean my character to take the blame. It was a tragedy for both Marisa and Bic."

"I didn't like dying. I was in love with you. And you killed me off just to be over the top dramatic."

"So, is that it, you came to my reality to kill me for revenge?"

"I'm not so hands on. If I wanted to kill you personally, I would have done it by now. I've got you in my crosshairs, Cory, and someone who you created will get to you. I promise you that."

"God, for a shrink and a rabbi, you're not so empathetic, are you? So, you're going to put a contract out on my life. Is that how you operate?"

"I know people Cory. Or have you forgotten the other characters you created. The former marine, Crazy Carl, my schizophrenic patient, Don, and the burglar?"

"Yes, but they are figments of my, MY imagination."

"Do you see me in the flesh, Cory. If that doesn't convince you that your banal characterizations and stilted dialogue have offended us all, then you don't deserve to call yourself a writer."

"Alright, so where does this leave me? What do you want an apology or something? You want me to join membership at your synagogue and give a hefty donation?"

"Your unyielding sarcasm is insolent," said Marisa.

"Your unjustifiable piety is nettling," I countered.

"You've been warned, you may have created us, but we can rid the world of you Cory Schulman." She got up and stormed out of the Starbucks. Just then, a sheepishly, bedraggled man entered Starbucks. He approached me at a high table.

"You know Mr. Schulman…I too am not happy with your depiction of me in *The Writer's Story*."

"Another one? You know my real name too."

"You wrote me in as a bumbling burglar. Ring a bell? It should. You created me but didn't even give me a name."

"Oh, yeah, well you weren't that integral to the story. To be honest, you were just an interjection to break up the monotony of the long conversation between the two protagonists."

"That's it, Schulman, or Luschman or Penman or whoever you want to be. If you created me as a nobody, I'll show you what a nobody crook I can be. This is your first and last warning. You better make sure your bedroom door is locked. You didn't even bother to give me a background story. Your characterization of me as a fool will catch up to you in the end.

Hear me now, you are a marked man. Start looking over your shoulder.”

“Okay, okay, you want a name, take Adolf.” I snorted inward.

“I’ll get you for that. You laugh at me now, but you’re the one who will get it in the end.”

“Hey Adolf. What if I just write you out of the story all together.”

“It’s too late Schulman. I’m here now. There’s no turning back.”

“Well then what if I just beat the hell out of you?”

He has a fit. “I’m not alone Schulman.”

“That’s what Marisa said. What does that mean anyway? Are all my discontented characters from my novel going to come after me?”

“Looks like it big shot. You created us in the worst possible light or put us in the worst situations. Call it literary karma. I’ll take your satchel now.”

“I call it bunk, little burglar man. What makes you think I’ll turn over my satchel?”

"Because I have a gun in my pocket pointed between your eyes."

"Why do you want this old thing? It's tearing apart. It's not good for anything."

You're right, it isn't, but what's inside is important. Your manuscript."

"How did you know that?"

"I came from your imagination. I know everything you are planning. Now hand it over."

"Wait a minute."

"I know you are days away from submitting it. This will hurt you, psychologically."

"I have copies of it you know? But here take it. I don't care."

The burglar took it and ran out the door yelling, "Do you have copies? Really? Check your basement room Schulman. I think you've been robbed."

Just then, I gulped in disappointment knowing that while I was sitting at the Starbucks, Adolf, as he is now known, must have robbed my room and snatched my computer.

"Damn. How did I get into this shit? How many more characters are coming to life to haunt me?"

On my way home, I ran into Prestogeorge. He immediately said, "We've been robbed. Or at least your stuff is missing. Unless you took it. Are you moving?"

"No," I said. And confirmed his suspicions, "I was robbed. And I know who did it."

"Are you going to call the police and report it?"

I'm taken back a bit. I can't very well contact the authorities without proper identification and my own shady background. Things would certainly unravel. They can't be involved at all. I simply replied curtly, "I'll handle it. No worries Prestogeorge." I went inside the row house and down into my basement room and sure enough, my laptop and other things were gone.

I pondered how I was going to deal with these ghosts of my own creation as well as my own ill-conceived marketing plan, which involved the tampering with Preston's body.

These characters and others will no doubt reveal who I am at the very least if not downright kill me. I need a plan to fight back, but I still have a day job that is keeping me afloat. So, I returned to the parlor and performed the jobs of a three member staff: cashiering, taking phone orders, preparing pizzas, and washing dishes.

By night's end, I was exhausted and smelled like an oven baked pizza. Marinara sauce seeped through my apron on to my regular clothes and a film of flower coated my forearms and face as well as oils, oregano, and shredded bits of mozzarella.

I needed to get my manuscript back and to get it within two days or my real reputation as a writer would be mud all over the book trade.

I considered who else may be after me, and then it hit me. Crazy Carl, the Viet Nam veteran grunt, or marine who was inflicted with PTSD.

I woke up the next day with clarity. I needed a gun. A weapon of some sort to defend myself. I wouldn't be able to ward off an ex-marine any other way. And if I had to shoot him, I would just flee the scene and pick up somewhere else.

I went to a local firearms store to buy a gun. I provided them with detailed identification information that I lifted from a previous employee of the pizza parlor. Little did I know, that employee had a police record, so I was denied the purchase of a real firearm. But the clerk suggested I could buy a bee bee rifle or a gun that shoots rubber bullets. I opted for the gun with non-lethal ammunition. I figured I could at least scare him or anybody else away with it. And I can avoid getting in any homicidal trouble.

I purchased the pistol and rubber bullets, then returned to my room. After I had fallen asleep, in the middle of the night, I awoke at the startling sound of a rock breaking my window. Then another rupture of a glass pane, as commando Crazy Carl slipped through the opening and cut his large belly on the remaining shards. He wore his full fatigues, which were now stained with blood from his entry.

I pulled out my gun, but Crazy Carl fearlessly charged me with his bare hands leading his assault. I didn't have time to say anything at all, no warnings, not stop or else; I just fired, fired, fired. The rubber bullets flitted through the gun barrel and found their target on his forehead, shoulder, and gut, which knocked him down. I approached him and aimed the gun directly against his eyeball and said, "Get out of here now and don't come back."

Crazy Carl limped away with throbbing muscle pain until he was no longer seen and exited the townhouse by way of the front door. Prestogeorge came running down the stairs, "What's going on down here?"

"Nothing, just getting rid of an intruder."

"Should I call the police?"

"No, the commotion is over."

"But should we call anyway and report it?"

"I said no. I'll handle it."

"I think I should report it. I can't take this anymore; someone is terrifying us. I can't live like this."

"They want me, not you Prestogeorge."

Then something weird changed in Prestogeorge. "Oh no, my demons, they're coming back."

I didn't know what the hell he was referring to until he mentioned cats with laser eyes. And suddenly I realized he was one of Marisa's schizophrenic patients. When he goes psychotic, he's a threat to everyone, including himself.

"You're one of them," he said. "You need to be destroyed," he asserted in a ghostly monotone."

"Crap, I'm even living with one of you imaginary lunatics."

Don Prestogeorge bulled toward me, but like a matador, I pivoted out of the way and he crashed headfirst into the wall, producing a divot into the drywall, the shape of his head. He retracted from the impression in the wall unscathed and charged once again. I whacked him on the back of the head with the butt of my gun and thrusted him to the side. And said, "I don't want to have to shoot you Don, and I know who you are. What's your beef?"

"You are a demon who must be destroyed before you take over the Earth."

Don was gone, his innocence replaced with hallucinations that only he believed in. I shouted at him, "You are experiencing a psychotic break. You can recognize it. Come back to me." But it was no use. No amount of rationale could debunk his belief that he was on a mission to kill demons. He menacingly got up again and this time jumped over the couch and leapt on top of me, but as we both fell to the floor, Don hit his head against a different wall made of brick and blacked out.

I got up and got the hell out of Dodge. I realized, there's no safe place for me here in the townhouse or at the pizza parlor, my cover was blown, and a team of individuals all saw their tortured existence as my fault.

I gathered my essentials and found a place to think. Not before long, I found myself at a park, populated with few passerbyers. My guard was up as anyone I confronted could be another disgruntled past character of mine. What was so ironic was that they all wanted to inflict harm onto the one who created them. Even Marisa, a rabbi and psychologist, who was supposed to embrace humanity was intolerant and wanted me dead. How can someone who pursues a life of piety also call for the demise of someone they had once loved? Something was askew. It just didn't make sense. She was so scornful. Perhaps that is it. A real person is complex, full of contradictions, and under severe stress and the right conditions become illogical, full of rage, and intolerant. Whereas my characters in my books are just fabrications of humanity, used for specific purposes that all pale in comparison to the protagonist. Real people can embrace a line of thinking that envelops them into a private bubble that is intolerant of any deviation or variation.

Compelled to escape the current barrage of insolent characters, I took the first bus out of this area. That happened to be in the direction of the Mid-West. I had to buy some time to reconsider my options.

I sat wedged between two other bus riders whose size suggested they eat little other than donuts. Once the bus arrived at a major depot, I got on another bus that was ready to go. I didn't care which direction I was going just so long it was far away from the chaos.

After crossing many states, I ended up in Mississippi, a part of the nation I've never experienced. As I was let off from the bus, I spotted a little tavern I believed would be a good resting stop. But as I walked from the road to the parking lot, more than a couple of Confederate flags hung off the backs of beat-up pickup trucks. They assaulted my retinas and peace of mind, but I was hungry and needed something to tide myself over until I could find a more respectable establishment.

With the greatest reluctance, I pulled open the front door expecting the worst. I immediately noticed that all the patrons were white. Although I was Caucasian, I felt very much out of place. Living in the DC metropolitan region all my life, I was accustomed to diversity, surrounded by international people, and cultured professionals of all persuasions.

My black-haired, Judaic appearance contrasted with the brown-haired "red necks" whose heritage was littered with generations of laborers dating back to the onset of the nation. These bearded patrons drank from pitchers of beer, one of whom placed his mug on his beer belly as if it were a table before taking another swallow. They drank and spoke cantankerously in a boisterous manner.

One of the men wore a tee shirt lettered with "Camp Auschwitz." They were celebrating their recent insurrection and storming of the nation's Capitol building in protest to the lost election results of the 2020 presidency. They, among an angry mob of thousands, smashed windows and bulled their way into the people's house and looted items from the desks of our legislators. They stole laptops, notebooks, and other articles as they rifled through desks and sat in prestigious Senate seats. Some had Malakoff cocktails, others had submachine guns and materials to bound hostages. Their invasion did temporarily stop the certification process of President-Elect Joe Biden as the legislators evacuated to a safe room for three hours until the unrest receded.

So, these guys are some of the members who acted on their beliefs shaped by conspiracy theories and inspired by the encouraging words of an inept president in his final days in office.

Then it hit me. Literary depictions of people need to be complex to be believable because real people are heavily flawed and contradictory. They go to church on Sunday and steal on Monday.

So, face to face with the white supremacists, I sat at a vacant table and felt compelled to stare at their spectacle, until one of them labored to a wobbly stand and grabbed his beer before trolling over to me.

My instinct was to leave before trouble broke out. But my obtuse cohort approached me and said, "What's a little faggot like you doing here?" He then poked me in the chest. So, I stood up. And he said, "There's no place for you here."

"Then I guess I'll get going."

He grabbed my wrist and twisted it. Off balance, I brought my leg up and hammered my foot on the side of his knee, which knocked him to the floor. His beer splashed and made a frothy puddle. While lying on his ass he brought up his head and slurred, "You Kike. You're mine now." As he got to his feet, I clubbed him with my fist, which stunned him, then I clubbed him in the head one more time and said, "This isn't Germany man, and it's no longer the 1930's. Go fuck off," and walked past the others who were about to get up, but I revealed my gun, the one that shot rubber bullets. They could not tell what kind of pistol it was, so I managed to get out of there unscathed.

As I left, I realized how simple it would have been to pull the trigger. I couldn't imagine having a real gun with lethal consequences. It would be too easy to shoot anyone you despised.

By night's end, I reflected on the opposites that flanked me this day. The emergence of overly righteous but scornful former girlfriend, who I gave life to from the recesses of my mind, and on the other side, these single-minded white supremacists who violated the sensibilities of our nation by claiming it for their own at the exclusion of others. Both driven by intolerance, zealousness, yet I'm equally intolerant of their stances. And given the chance, if there were no consequences to my actions, I would easily get rid of them all. I suppose this element of intolerance is a part of everyone, no matter how distasteful a quality it is.

Then I realized, I may have no influence in the real world to persuade those ignoramuses from the tavern, but I can influence my characters by rewriting them, giving them depth and qualities of conscience and doubt. They don't need to be cardboard cutouts but carry with them the capacity to be and do anything. They can have unpredictability, conclusions based on the confluence of circumstance, motivation, reason, and heart.

After several weeks, I returned to my basement room in Maryland, knowing that I was an easy target from my own insurrected characters. They want change, I'll give them change. I took out my newly purchased replacement laptop and started rewriting *The Writer's Story*. I began with Don Prestogeorge since he was all over the map crashing his head into walls. I rewrote his passages to include his taking a regimen of psychotropic medication. I prescribed him Vraylar, which should mitigate his psychotic episodes within days. No longer would he fear cats with laser vision or be unable to discern the real from his delusions.

Second, I revised Crazy Carl to be more meditative to combat his PTSD. I removed his bitterness toward the government and re-instilled a great sense of patriotism so that he would stand by to serve and protect his countrymen.

For the burglar, I gave him a name: Larry, and I concocted a scene where he won the lottery, which diminished his compelling need to steal and rob.

Lastly, I dug deep down to bring Marisa's character to a well-rounded fruition. I instilled a sense of logic and appreciation of earth-bound things and experiences, with less reliance on the supernatural faith or reliance on psychological training. And altered the ending of her demise from choking on an ice cube. Now she survives that episode and is no longer in peril.

Just then, Marisa peered through the basement window and knocked on it. Do I dare let her in. But the fact is to resolve any of this uprising, I must face the faults of my own character development of these cast members. I decided to let her in.

Marisa, cool as a cat, strutted in wearing her high heeled boots and tightly covered skirt and leather jacket. She lifted up her opaque shades and glared at me. "Well, I see someone has been doing some homework. Don is feeling better, Carl reinstated himself into the national reserves, and the burglar is out shopping instead of stealing."

"Yeah, well what about you, Marisa? Are we good now that I made your character survive?"

"Not exactly, Cory Schulman aka Bic Penman, there's the little matter between us."

"There's nothing between us — other than you are a disobedient character from my imagination who's come to life to haunt me for my own limitations to write credible works of literature. Supposedly, I have rectified the matter with revisions to my work, rendering your presence here unnecessary. I've acquiesced to your point of view and have addressed the issues at hand. You have survived the choking incident, which of course, undermines the entire premise of *The Writer's Story* — making it into a pointless story, for if Marisa, your character, doesn't die then Bic Penman can't be arrested for murder."

"Or," Marisa interjected, "You could continue rewriting and have us get married, making the ultimate bridge between my character of faith and emotion with your character of logic and atheism."

"Never, Marisa. As you know my position on marriage is that it is a formality to create the illusion of permanency when nothing is so, and such a union will only last for as long as each member sees value and commits to such an agreement.”

“That leaves me no choice then. I will have to call the authorities and reveal your morbid little secret.”

“YOU wouldn’t.”

“I can and I will.”

“You are blackmailing me in order to marry me? Doesn’t the coercion part of blackmailing a person conflict with the ‘love you until death do us part’ thing of marriage?”

“You have my conditions. Marriage, or you are outed.”

“What if I out myself and just confess?”

“Do you really want to take the risk of relying on faith that people will believe you?”

“Yeah, you do know me well enough to call my bluff. But the deception has to end at some point. That’s the impetus of the crime in the first place. To call attention to myself and sell more books. To become a part of the national conversation. To make a mark on society that indicates that I was here and made some sort of impact.”

"Do you think Preston's family will see it that way? They are still worrying without a clue to where their loved one is. They've filed a missing person's report."

"I guess you got me there. I didn't think through all of the ramifications of my actions. It was an impulsive action. The whole switching of the identifications. Look Marisa, I guess I should be flattered in a way that you want to marry me, but can't you just be satisfied with not dying?"

"Can't you just be satisfied with just getting married?"

"I thought the point of marriage is to have reciprocating motivations to engage in such a ritual. Therefore, to force someone to marry them is contradictory to its nature and purpose."

"I expect you'll come to your senses after deep reflection of the true, universal values. So, I'll leave you with that thought and await your answer."

I did come to my senses, which brought me a swell of pride and confidence. If Marisa thought she could blackmail me, she thought wrong. Since at some point I would have to reveal the truth to get on with my life, why not now. I would take away Marisa's leverage by outing myself before she did. It was time to end the charade.

But how to do it without punishment. That would be impossible, but I could get one last marketing bang for my buck. I called every national news source and told them that the perpetrator to the Schulman case will be revealed at Times Square at 8:00 am right at the time the morning news programs are televised live.

Some of the reporters believed this to be a dangerous proposition, thinking a bomb may be detonated. That unintentional implication invited an even greater focus on my plan. The news entities naturally contacted the authorities which brought a S.W.A.T. team and bomb sniffing canines to the scene. As chaotic as the Times Square intersection is under ordinary times, it was hyper intensified with my antics.

So, with another 15 minutes of fame to gain and everything else to lose, at 8:00 am I strolled out to the middle of the intersection where cars honked at me and whooshed by. I upheld a large white sign that read "Cory Schulman is alive" then walked toward a cameraman so that it could be seen nationally. Soon a mob surrounded me, asking questions; I dropped my sign as I became buried with onlookers. The mob became rowdy which was incentive enough to try to slip away. Just as I emerged from the crowd, I was greeted by a German Shephard showing incisors ready to really dismember me. Three S.W.A.T. agents were behind the guard dog and they closed on me as if I were a terrorist. I was now caught.

***

In custody, I first had to make a statement that I was, indeed, Cory Schulman, the author of *The Writer's Story*. Secondly, I had to prove that my statement was true. I provided my fingerprints,

313

and an officer swabbed the inside of my cheek for a DNA analysis. The authorities then recorded my confession, at least all that I disclosed. I held back some information, such as whose beheaded body was actually found in my crashed vehicle. I believed that I could reveal this information in exchange for a plea bargain.

After a couple of days behind bars, I was let go on my own recognizance, but with a court date. So, I hired a lawyer and negotiated, bargained, pleaded, and begged, which didn't get me a lot of sympathy, but after cashing in on my bargaining chip to reveal Preston's identity and therefore solve his missing person's case, I was able to obtain immunity on the most serious of my crimes.

Despite the legal fees, fines, and being on probation for about the rest of my life, I was now a known author. Although quasi famous, no one would hire me. My retirement savings were depleted to satisfy legal fees and fines. And in the twilight of the night, I thought that it would have been far easier to have had spent my assets on professional marketing groups. I may have accomplished the same sales results without the morbidity that lingers in my mind every night, the shame of causing the Preston family any pain, and the expense of the trial.

After extensive legal wrangling and throwing myself on the mercy of the court, I did escape incarceration. But I had to use one more bargaining chip that I really didn't want to use: Marisa. Who would have thought that I barely escaped imprisonment because of Marisa, who agreed to be my character witness and was the difference in serving time? Of course, this sudden cooperation from her came with a condition that we wed.

So, we went to the courthouse again, but this time to get legally married. At first, Marisa proved to be a good wife, except when she read my drafts of novels. In those cases, she became my most stringent critic, nettling me with superficial punctuation complaints. But what could I expect from someone who never really had a real life? She was right in one respect; I did create superficial characters with skinny background stories.

My marriage to Marisa made our attendance to my 20-year high school reunion all that much more challenging in that everybody one meets at a reunion wants to either reminisce about the times of yesteryear or learn everything about you. We expected the "Where did you meet your spouse?" question to cause us the most consternation.

How would I, we, address that one? I had no idea. If I told the truth, it would go something like, I wrote a novel with banal characters who rebelled against their superficial characterizations by coming to life to exact revenge on me, which I prevented by agreeing to marry my protagonist.

As for the "What do you do for a living?" question. If not already known from my notorious past, I would have to explain, I was a failed novelist who sought attention and benefits from sensational news that I died in a gruesome murder, which I staged, ultimately had to confess to the misdeed, and spent every penny of my estate to avoid imprisonment.

When Marisa and I arrived at Gaithersburg High School, we first congregated with other attendees, none of whom I recognized. In the nucleus of the small gathering, a tour guide called everyone's attention and formally introduced himself as Keith, a 40-year-old PE teacher at the school. After covering his history with the school, he explained that the class of 2001 had about 200 graduates and that about 60 of them and their spouses had RSVP'd that they were coming to the night's dinner and dancing event.

Keith led the group of about 25 alumni and their significant others to refresh their memories of the school and to see the changes that have been done during the past 20 years. The tour guide led our group from the entrance, which he pointed out was rebuilt a decade after we had graduated. Walking through the same halls that we did 20 years ago was surreal, as if we could see ghosts of our former, underdeveloped teenager selves. It was as if each locker was a former student, all skin and bones with the same hair styles. From the perspective of a different era, we had all looked the same, no different than our tall, skinny lockers.

As Keith led the tour along various hallways, rooms, the auditorium, cafeteria, each part of the school ushered in memories, some good, some bad, most inconsequential. Then the tour turned the corner into a brightly lit hallway, titled the Hall of Fame. This hallway had the potential to devastate the weak at heart. The guide explained that alumni who have made a significant contribution to society are glorified with a plaque of their image in bronze relief and their short biography. Plaques of students from nearly every year since the inception of the high school honored their achievements, which included those who became professional athletes, television personalities, celebrities, politicians, and so forth.

Just before we exited the Hall of Fame, I see one name I recognize from our year of graduation: Daniel Grover. A sudden wave of ambivalence overtook me at the sight of my own peer group honored as if immortal. A whiff of pride was overshadowed with envy and general feeling of nausea as if I were drinking a strawberry smoothie mixed with refried beans. The two feelings just didn't go together naturally.

How could I have such a visceral reaction to someone else I knew some 20 years ago. Then it hit me. It isn't so much about him as it was about how I felt about myself. In fact, I realized, this whole reunion wasn't about anyone other than me and how I faired in comparison.

As the group followed the leader down the corridor to the next wing, I picked out my phone from my pocket and entered Daniel Grover's name in the search field. A page of links displayed, even Wikipedia. He actually had a profile in Wikipedia. It listed him as an American Physicist who published an array of papers on the nature of light and things I could barely comprehend. Was he that bright? He was such a pill when I knew him. A dork, socially vanilla.

Then the contrast came to light. While I floundered emotionally and academically during high school, obsessing about girls, he was getting academic scholarships to Ivy league schools where, despite the intense competition and rigorous criteria, he shined. The thought of meeting him in person at the night activities made me notice that I was breathing heavily through my mouth. I could only think that while my greatest accomplishment was to write a few novels, he was solving life's eternal riddles. I realized that I will always live in fiction while people like Daniel will always live in the throes of reality.

***

I did find the courage to attend the nighttime activities. We all gathered in a private room of a local hotel where the reality of meeting former students and their spouses after 20 years was a deadening intrusion of the senses. The few students that I knew of back in the day were only recognizable by their picture of their former selves taped to their chest. Everybody was older now. Carrying too much weight. Thinning and receding hairlines instead of a mop of hair that touched their shoulders. The women too, overweight, all had stomachs that blended with their bosoms. Long gone were their sexy hourglass waists and narrow hips. The skintight jeans were replaced with long dresses that draped over the moguls of fat. Their faces no longer sharp edged. Yes, everyone was facing middle age.

The reunion either took one back to a time when we were boundless with time in front of us and/or was a terrible reminder of the time that has passed and placed us closer to the nothingness of death.

The mix of what makes people embrace life is astonishing. To some, they need to show wealth through material acquisition. To others, it's the pride they have in their kids. To others it's social standing, the name droppers. The toppers seem to want to be better than anything mentioned.

Most, like myself become the vanillas: teachers, restaurant managers, accountants. Somehow each of us spill out of the carton of milk, and like an unwiped spill, sit on the countertop shrinking from evaporation until we are nothing. How can anyone change their disposition at this point? Youth, health, and time have all evaporated.

So, Marisa and I found ourselves mingling amongst strangers and their even more unfamiliar spouses. The alcohol helped deaden the hypersensitivity of our egos until it was clearly understood that no one attending belonged on the Hall of Fame. We were all vanillas.

Reunions are all about exaggerating the truth or revealing the truth. It just depends on one's insecurity level and how it plays off the integrity of who you meet at these reunions. I was penniless, shamed, and pressured into marriage, but proud none the less because I remained true to my core nature. I may have caved in marrying Marisa as a quid pro quo to get her positive testimony of my character during the trial, but I then refused to change the ending of my novel. I am a storyteller, and whether I tell my stories without pecuniary success, I remain who I am. But the attention I did get from killing myself through a false scenario did give me a piece of action: my 15 minutes in the spotlight. Although I will have to defend my actions for the rest of my life. In a way, I've given everyone a reason to become my critic, even my wife.

As I ruminated the meaning of my life, eventually Marisa and I found ourselves among a small crowd. Just as discussions of kids and sad stories of divorce and diabetes, knee and hip pain, back pain, couldn't be any less excruciating, some of the issues that I had been obsessing about were being brought up by others too. So, I tossed in my three cents of wisdom, "In the end, does it really matter what others think of you? The question isn't can you impress anyone; it's whether you can impress yourself in a life that you, and only you, answer to. You create your meaning for your life."

This brought about a sharp rebuke by Lois, who I didn't know from a hole in the wall, "You sound as if you live in your own bubble. We don't though. Our lives are intertwined with others whether we like it or not. What you do affects others and other people's actions affect you. We're a society."

Then a guy named Darryl Gloober, who I also didn't know said, "You have to have pride in something like being the best at something."

Not to be left out of a good philosophical reflection, Darin Macoby offered a cynical contribution, "You're only as good as your last accomplishment."

His wife chimed into a different tune, "We just need to participate in life, not be the best." And before you knew it, everybody had an opinion, which were all derivative of some cliché.

"It's different for everybody. Some need to be movers and shakers, others just sit back and watch the world go by."

"That's silly, I have pride in my children regardless of whether I'm the best parent in the world."

"You have pride in procreation? Yeah, like that's an incredible unprecedented accomplishment."

"I have eight kids and I wouldn't know what I would have to live for without them."

"I think the things that satisfy us in life changes over time as our priorities change."

"She's right, during my boyhood, sports and winning mattered more than anything. During adolescence, a clear complexion and maturing physique took over, then its physical gratification, popularity. Now all I care about is a hot cup of coffee in the morning and peace and quiet at home while I read the headlines."

"It's not being the best, or even good at something, or having something like a big house, fancy car, or prestigious job. It's all about integrity. Let's drink to that!" As everyone in our coterie raised their mugs, a sudden flash of memory came to light. Upon hearing those words, 'Let's drink to that,' I recognized the woman next to me. She was Judy Macintyre, the one who was mortified those many years ago. I leaned over to her, compelled by a sense of duty, and softly disclosed "By the way, it was the quarterback, Marty Barest, who urinated into your beer mug that you drank." Judy's eyes bulged as the memory came thrusting to the forefront of her consciousness. Her stomach wrenched; she gagged on the real beer she was about to swallow, feeling as if it were indeed the urine she swallowed in front of her peers twenty years ago. Then she projectile vomited into the crowd, soaking the former quarterback. She then screamed at him and punched him in the chest several times. The quarterback shoved her to the floor, which provoked someone else to turn on the former athlete and before you knew it, people were freewheeling punching and tackling each and everybody in a melee that did prove we are all intertwined.

Marisa and I ducked out of the bar room and entered a different, more peaceful lounge area where I finally met someone else who I recognized, Suskia Sudhaven. I had been sweet on her during high school, but never had the depth to broach the silence between us. And she looked pretty damn good twenty years later. After a pleasant greeting and introduction to my wife, we three began to chat for the first time.

"So, you two are married? How did you meet?"

I couldn't very well tell Suskia that I met Marisa when I concocted her from my imagination. But I could say the truth without it sounding so far-fetched. I finally offered, "We met through our mutual appreciation of literature. Our shared interest in story telling is our story." Then it hit me. Just tell the beginning of our relationship as it unfolded in *The Writer's Story*. "We met through an online dating site, Date Now. Our first meeting was at a Starbucks where we pretty much disagreed on everything, but noticed we were still enraptured with one another. After a few years, we decided to make it official and tied the noose, I mean knot."

She gives a conflicted look. Then asked, "What do you do Marisa?"

"I'm a rabbi and a psychologist."

"Really, women can become rabbis? I didn't know that."

"Not all segments of Judaism recognize women rabbis, but I just need acceptance from my own congregation."

"That would drive me crazy," Suskia confessed.

"Well, I'm a psychologist too. So, I can address the psychological impact at the same time I preach God's word."

Suskia appeared conflicted again. "Well, you two seem like a perfect match."

"Yeah, who would have thought an atheist would ever marry a rabbi. But if there's ever a time we drive each other nuts, we just undergo a therapy session. I even get the spousal discount," I tried to introduce humor into the otherwise contradiction.

"You know Cory," Suskia admitted, "Back in the day, I had a secret crush on you."

"Really. I was quite found of you too. But back then, I was too shy to approach the ladies."

"We lived right near each other. We would pass each other every day on the sidewalk on our way to school. You were so cute. And we shared homeroom together because our last names both started with S. In fact, we shared homeroom together for five years since the seventh grade. And we worked at places that were right next to each other. Remember, I was a hairdresser and you worked in the pizza restaurant."

"Wow you remember everything."

"I remember you not saying a word for those five years."

"Like I said, I didn't know how to talk to people back then. So, tell me something about your life. Are you still local?"

"No, I moved back to my mother's homeland in Sweden. I'm just back to visit family and friends."

"That's pretty far off. I stayed local for the most part. I went to state college and bought a home in the city."

"So, what does the mostly local mean? Where else did you go?"

"Oh, well that's kind of my x-file. I was a fugitive for a while after I faked my own death in a lame scheme to generate publicity for my literary works. I was all over the country until I got tired of working for minimum wage. I worked in a car wash, pizza restaurants, book shops, I was a sign twirler for a mattress discounter. I served as a truck loader. Just the worst jobs for someone my age with a college degree. I mean those types of jobs were fine when we were 15 or so, but now not so much."

"So, what happened? Did you sell a lot of books? Get arrested?"

"I did sell a lot of books, but the royalties all went to pay legal fees. And I did avoid imprisonment because of my sparkly clean record and the fact that I tried to help a man in a car accident with CPR to no avail. And I helped them solve the missing persons case that I created when I stole the man's identity."

"So, you've been busy since high school. That's a colorful history."

"In a way it's ironic that I pulled this death prank as an educated person, while in high school, I never participated in any pranks. You could say that I've made a name for myself."

Then Marisa interjected, "Which one would that be: Roy C. Luschman or Cory Schulman, or Bic Penman?"

"Alright, so I've made several names for myself. I'm only 38 and notoriously known. Failings build character."

Marisa rebutted, "And we all agree that you have a lot of character."

Suskia returned to Cory, "What are you going to do from now on, for the rest of your working years?"

"I'll go as far as my imagination takes me. If there are any more books in me, I'll write them," I said.

"You can support yourself as a novelist?" Suskia asked.

"Well, I am married to a woman who holds two jobs."

"She's willing to support you?"

"While my future as a writer appears dismal, I do have faith in Marisa."

"What about you. Won't you feel bad if your wife is earning all the money?" Suskia asked suggesting her own conservative expectations.

"She kind of owes me. I sort of made her who she is."

"And now you're married."

"Yeah, well you can't win them all."

"Don't tell me you don't care for your marriage."

"To be honest, I had always dreamt of marrying you."

"Me?"

"I never forgot you."

"Well, you made your decision," Suskia shot back trying to defray the embarrassment.

"I did write my own script and now I have to live with it. The reunion is dwindling down to just a few. I guess it will soon be over. Since you're in town, would you like to come visit Marisa and me for dinner at our house tomorrow?"

Since she was in town for just a couple of days without any other plans, Suskia accepted the invitation, but caveated that she didn't have a car. I said, "No worries Suskia, I can pick you up from your hotel and drive you to our house."

***

The next day I picked up Suskia from her hotel and drove her to my home. On the way, Suskia asked again about me and Marisa, "So you found love again with Marisa, Cory?"

I couldn't help but hesitate, giving away a truth about my marriage to Marisa. Finally surrendering to proper etiquette, I answered glibly, "Yeah, Marisa's great."

"You should be more excited than that Cory. You just got married. You two are newlyweds. That's the most magical time in a marriage, when everything goes right and nothing bothers you. You should be buoyed by the inspiration of love," she tried to poetically persuade me.

Then I tried to explain in a succinct manner: "I guess it's just complicated being middle aged and getting married again. It's not the same as the first time."

"Then why did you do it?"

"Marisa and I go back a long way. We have a unique relationship. She's perfect, not a single flaw." Then I tried to deflect the attention, "What's your situation? Have you ever been married Suskia?"

"Yes, but my husband died from a brain tumor a few years ago."

"Sorry to hear that Suskia," I offered my sympathies.

"He was a great husband. I miss him."

On that sad note, we turned on to my street and parked in the driveway. I got out and, with some chivalry, I walked around to the other side of the car and opened Suskia's passenger door.

We entered the house hearing sounds of squeaking springs and grunts and moans coming from the bedroom. We immediately suspected some devious sexual escapade. We followed the sounds to the bedroom and, with full expectations of seeing either a breach of our wedding vows or a horrific rape, I pushed open the door. All we could see were the sheet covers shrouding two bodies thrusting and retracting rhythmically. This was no rape. They were both enjoying the interlude. I yelled out, "Hey" and the action below the covers ceased and Marisa's face poked up horrified at being caught in the middle of intercourse.

"Infidelity? Really Marisa, really you and…" Then the other head popped out from beneath the covers. He craned his neck and looked at me with equal surprise.

"Don? Don the schizophrenic? One of your patients? Your one act of infidelity is in violation of so many aspects of your two professions. I just don't know what you were thinking. Why did you want to marry me in the first place if you were going to be unfaithful?"

"I can explain. Just give me a chance. Cory." As Marisa's lover extricated himself from her and, with her arm across her bare breasts, Marisa bent over to pick up her clothes. "People are complex. We don't always act the same way in all situations like cardboard pieces to a game. We have needs, instincts, choices, God the choices, and opportunities. Like your decision to lop off Preston's head."

As Suskia and I watched Marisa frantically dressing herself, I shook my head and yelled back, "Don't throw this back on me Marisa. You were the one who wanted to get married. You are the one bound, or at least I thought you were, to higher religious and ethical standards. And you commit adultery in the first weeks of our marriage, a marriage you coerced upon me."

"But don't you see? You and I are the same. We are just thrown into life and must grapple with the circumstances for our entire lives without it meaning any more than what we make it."

"That's your defense: taking no responsibility for your actions?"

"All I'm saying is that, while we pray to God, we aren't God; we aren't perfect. That's what we were trying to tell you by coming alive out of your book *The Writer's Story*. To be an effective writer, your characters must have depth and complexity and yes contradictions because if you want to convince anyone that your writing has a sense of reality, you must present characters with true dimension. To reflect reality, we must be flawed."

About the Author

Cory Schulman is a native Marylander and an author of seven books. Shortly after earning his B.A. degree in psychology from Salisbury State College, he established a writing firm which he managed for 15 years. Mr. Schulman then worked as a Technical Writer for global federal contractors for the following 20 years. He has also taught technical writing part-time at a local college and is currently working on a non-fiction book on art fundamentals.

www.ingramcontent.com/pod-product-compliance
Lightning Source LLC
Chambersburg PA
CBHW072202130726
47910CB00011B/1786